W9-ATS-763

THE RESCUE ADVENTURE OF STENNY GREEN,
HINDENBURG CRASH EYEWITNESS

BY **CANDICE RANSOM**
ADAPTATION BY **EMMA CARLSON BERNE**
ILLUSTRATED BY **TED HAMMOND** AND **RICHARD PIMENTEL CARBAJAL**

Graphic Universe™ Minneapolis • New York

# INTRODUCTION

THE *HINDENBURG* WAS A GERMAN ZEPPELIN. ZEPPELINS WERE AIRSHIPS THAT LOOKED SIMILAR TO BALLOONS AND BLIMPS. BUT UNLIKE A BALLOON OR A BLIMP, A ZEPPELIN HAD A RIGID FRAME THAT HELPED IT KEEP ITS SHAPE. A ZEPPELIN'S FRAME WAS COVERED WITH HEAVY, WATERPROOFED CLOTH. THE CLOTH COVERS HAD POCKETS FILLED WITH HYDROGEN GAS. HYDROGEN IS LIGHTER THAN THE AIR IN THE ATMOSPHERE, SO A ZEPPELIN FILLED WITH HYDROGEN FLOATED.

THE *HINDENBURG* WAS A MASSIVE CRAFT—MORE THAN 803 FEET LONG. ITS OWNERS HAD HIGH HOPES OF BEGINNING REGULARLY SCHEDULED FLIGHTS BETWEEN GERMANY AND THE UNITED STATES. CROSSING THE ATLANTIC OCEAN TOOK THE ZEPPELIN TWO OR THREE DAYS.

THIS WAS QUICKER THAN EVEN THE FASTEST OCEAN LINER, WHICH TOOK AT LEAST FIVE DAYS. THE *HINDENBURG* MADE ITS FIRST FLIGHT IN 1936. THAT YEAR, THE ZEPPELIN MADE 17 SUCCESSFUL ROUND-TRIP FLIGHTS, INCLUDING 10 LANDINGS IN LAKEHURST, NEW JERSEY. THE AIRSHIP CARRIED MORE THAN 3,500 PASSENGERS. THE FIRST NORTH AMERICAN FLIGHT OF 1937 WAS SCHEDULED TO ARRIVE AT LAKEHURST IN MAY.

DISASTER STRUCK ON MAY 6, 1937. THE *HINDENBURG* BURST INTO FLAMES ABOVE THE LANDING FIELD IN LAKEHURST AND FELL TO THE GROUND. ALTHOUGH THE CHARACTERS IN THIS STORY ARE FICTIONAL, THE EVENTS THEY WITNESSED ARE TRUE.

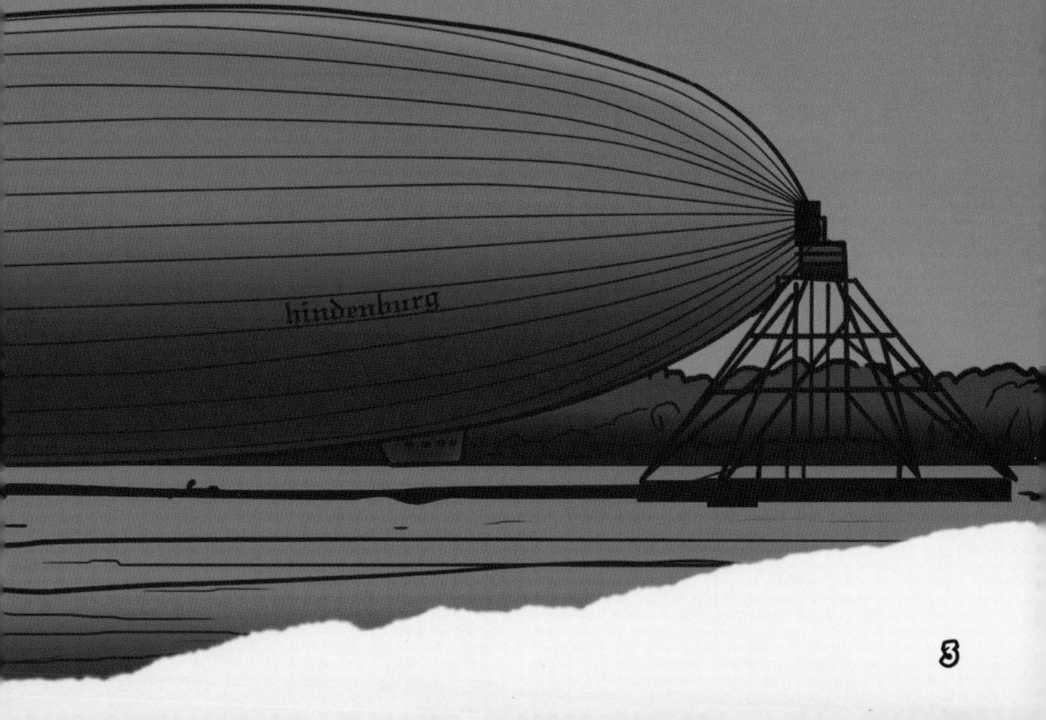
hindenburg

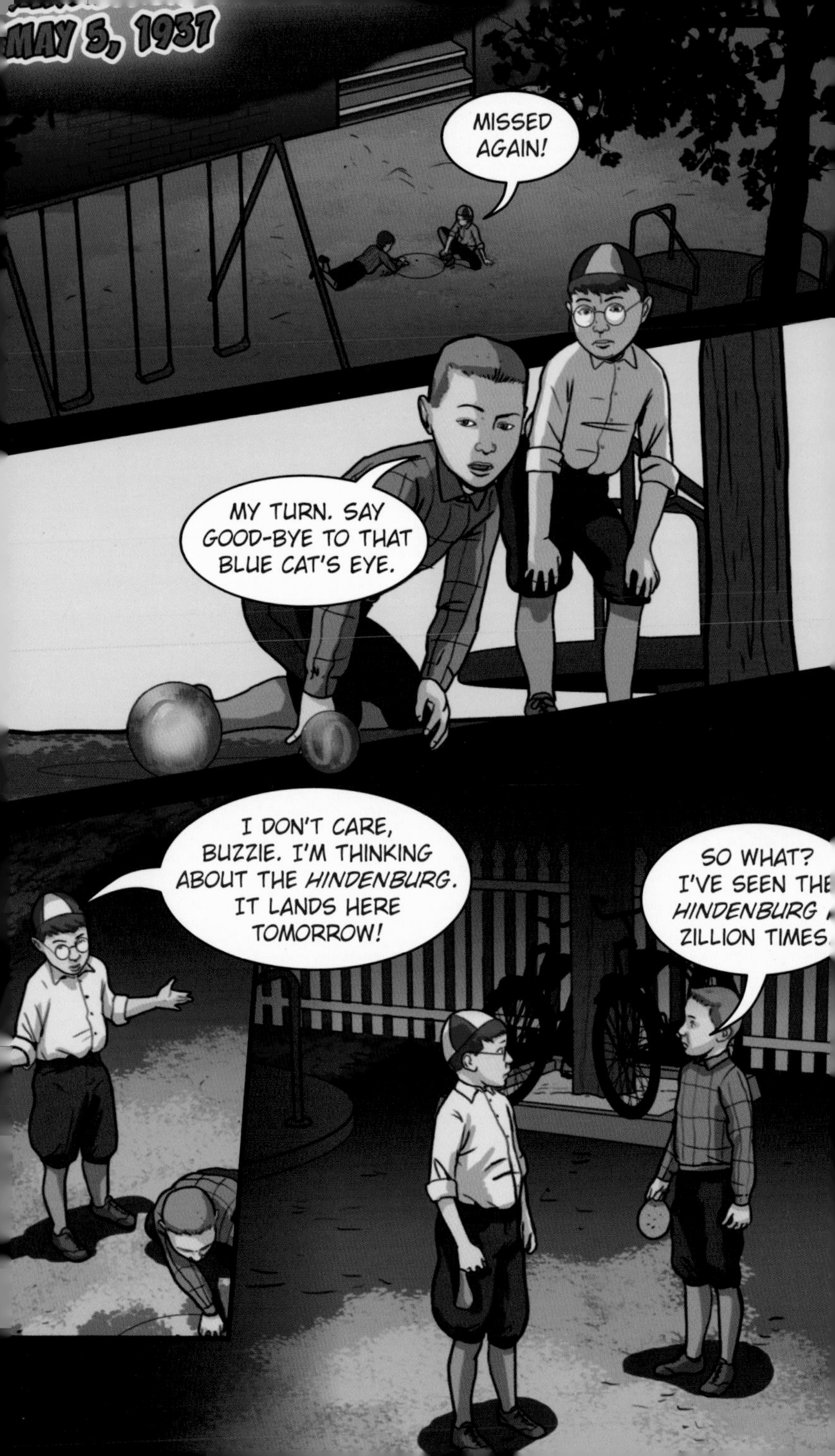
MAY 5, 1937
MISSED AGAIN!
MY TURN. SAY GOOD-BYE TO THAT BLUE CAT'S EYE.
I DON'T CARE, BUZZIE. I'M THINKING ABOUT THE *HINDENBURG*. IT LANDS HERE TOMORROW!
SO WHAT? I'VE SEEN THE *HINDENBURG* A ZILLION TIMES.

MY BROTHER IS GOING TO GET ME A SPECIAL PASS TO GET ON THE *HINDENBURG* TOMORROW.
YOU SAID THAT LAST YEAR. AND YOU NEVER GOT ON IT.
WELL, LAST YEAR MICHAEL WAS BUSY.
MICHAEL, STENNY'S 19-YEAR-OLD BROTHER, WAS AN ENLISTED MAN AT THE NAVAL AIR STATION. HE WAS STUDYING TO BECOME AN AIRSHIP NAVIGATOR.
SEE YOU IN SCHOOL TOMORROW!
I MAY BE LATE! I DON'T KNOW HOW LONG THAT TOUR WILL TAKE. MAYBE THREE OR FOUR HOURS!

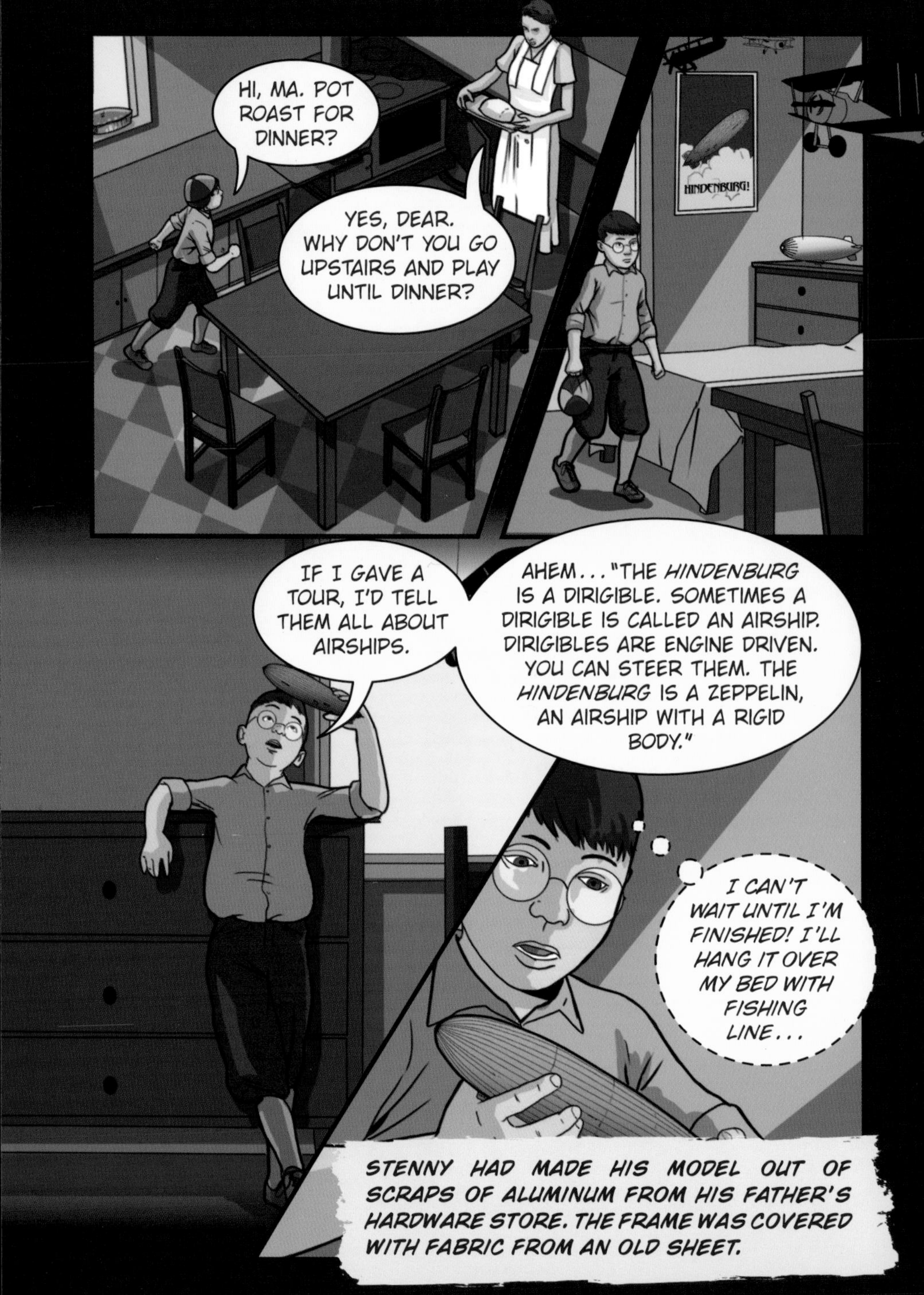
HI, MA. POT ROAST FOR DINNER?
YES, DEAR. WHY DON'T YOU GO UPSTAIRS AND PLAY UNTIL DINNER?
HINDENBURG!
IF I GAVE A TOUR, I'D TELL THEM ALL ABOUT AIRSHIPS.
AHEM . . . "THE *HINDENBURG* IS A DIRIGIBLE. SOMETIMES A DIRIGIBLE IS CALLED AN AIRSHIP. DIRIGIBLES ARE ENGINE DRIVEN. YOU CAN STEER THEM. THE *HINDENBURG* IS A ZEPPELIN, AN AIRSHIP WITH A RIGID BODY."
I CAN'T WAIT UNTIL I'M FINISHED! I'LL HANG IT OVER MY BED WITH FISHING LINE . . .
STENNY HAD MADE HIS MODEL OUT OF SCRAPS OF ALUMINUM FROM HIS FATHER'S HARDWARE STORE. THE FRAME WAS COVERED WITH FABRIC FROM AN OLD SHEET.

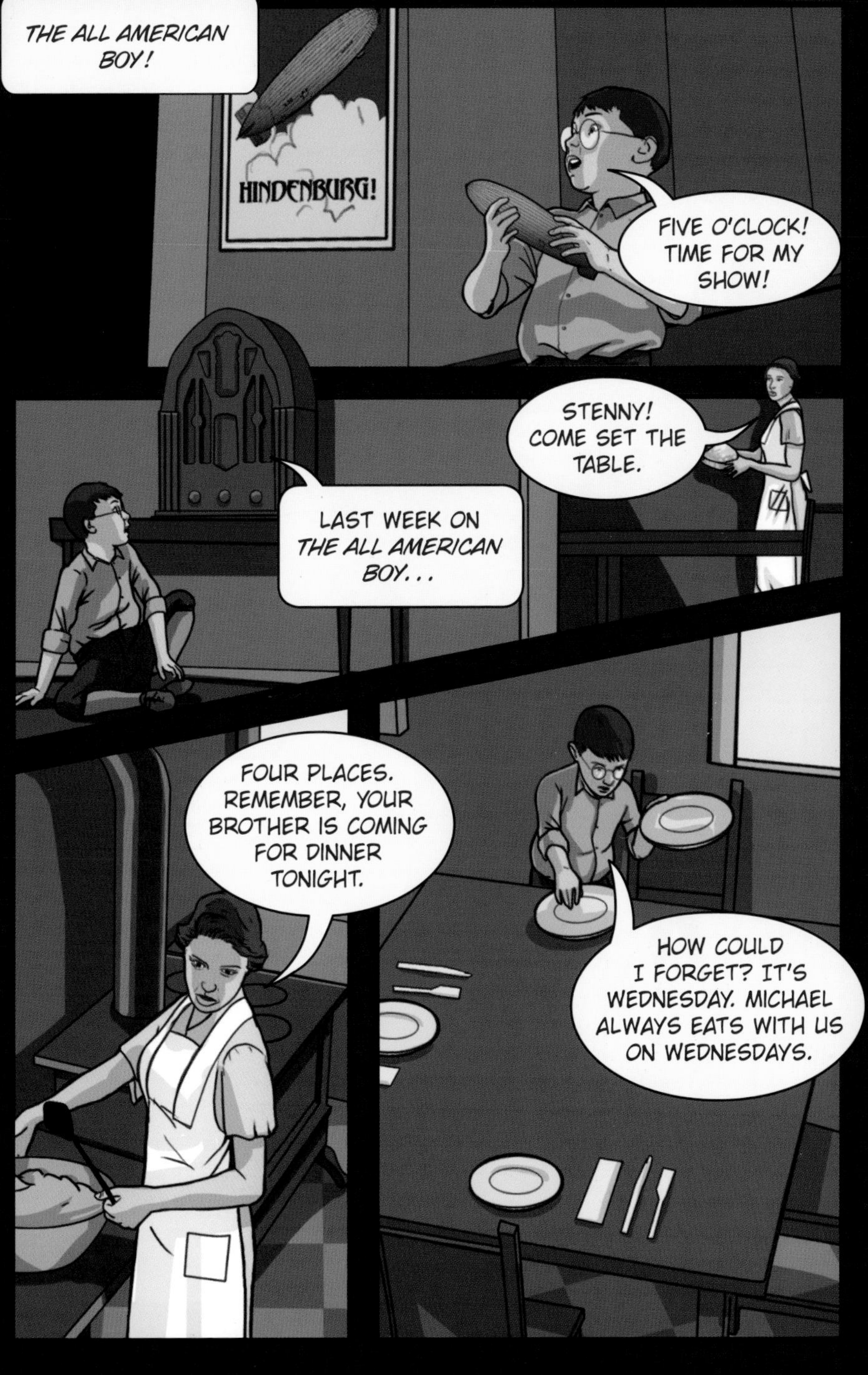
THE ALL AMERICAN BOY!
HINDENBURG!
FIVE O'CLOCK! TIME FOR MY SHOW!
STENNY! COME SET THE TABLE.
LAST WEEK ON THE ALL AMERICAN BOY. . .
FOUR PLACES. REMEMBER, YOUR BROTHER IS COMING FOR DINNER TONIGHT.
HOW COULD I FORGET? IT'S WEDNESDAY. MICHAEL ALWAYS EATS WITH US ON WEDNESDAYS.

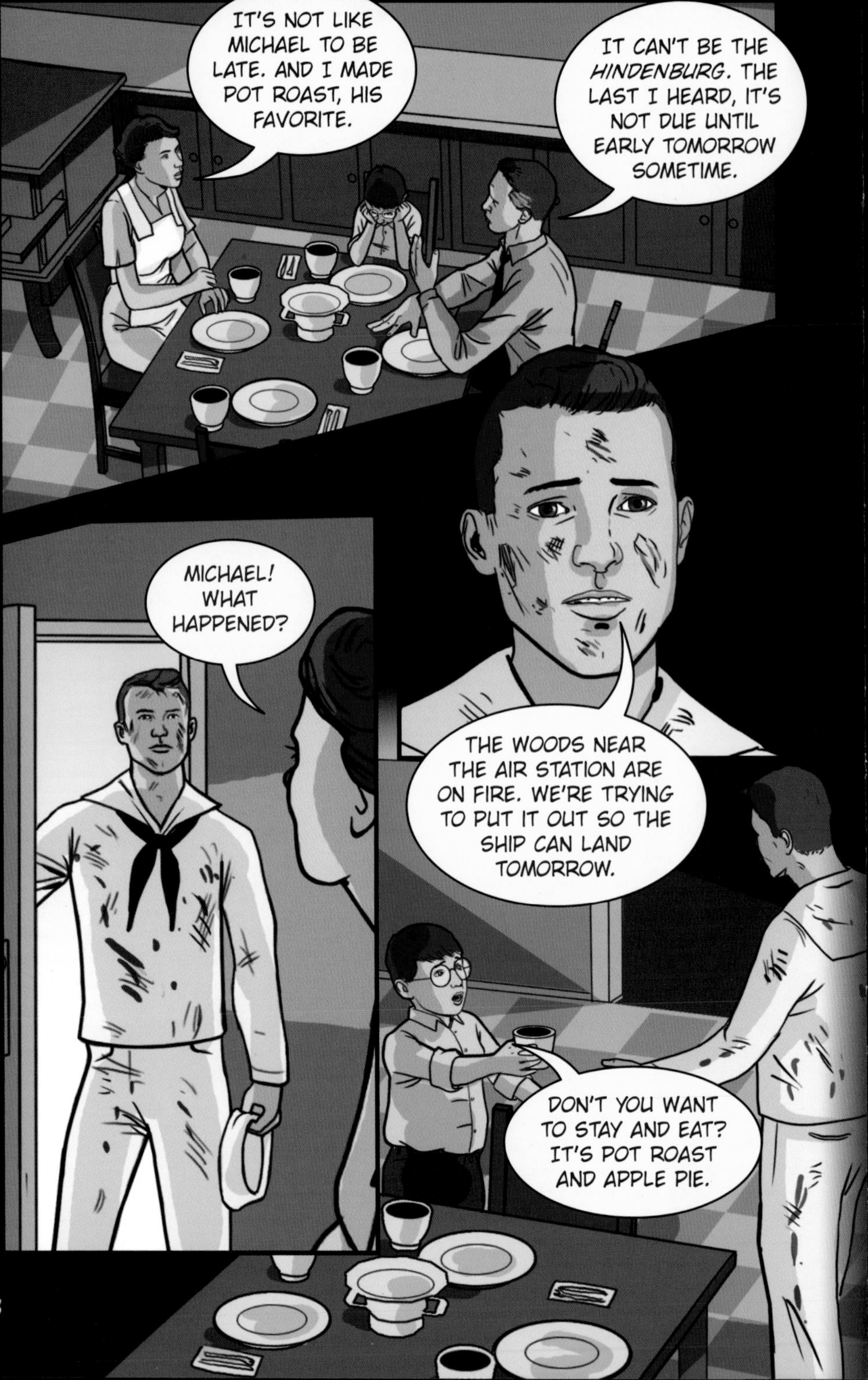
IT'S NOT LIKE MICHAEL TO BE LATE. AND I MADE POT ROAST, HIS FAVORITE.
IT CAN'T BE THE *HINDENBURG*. THE LAST I HEARD, IT'S NOT DUE UNTIL EARLY TOMORROW SOMETIME.
MICHAEL! WHAT HAPPENED?
THE WOODS NEAR THE AIR STATION ARE ON FIRE. WE'RE TRYING TO PUT IT OUT SO THE SHIP CAN LAND TOMORROW.
DON'T YOU WANT TO STAY AND EAT? IT'S POT ROAST AND APPLE PIE.

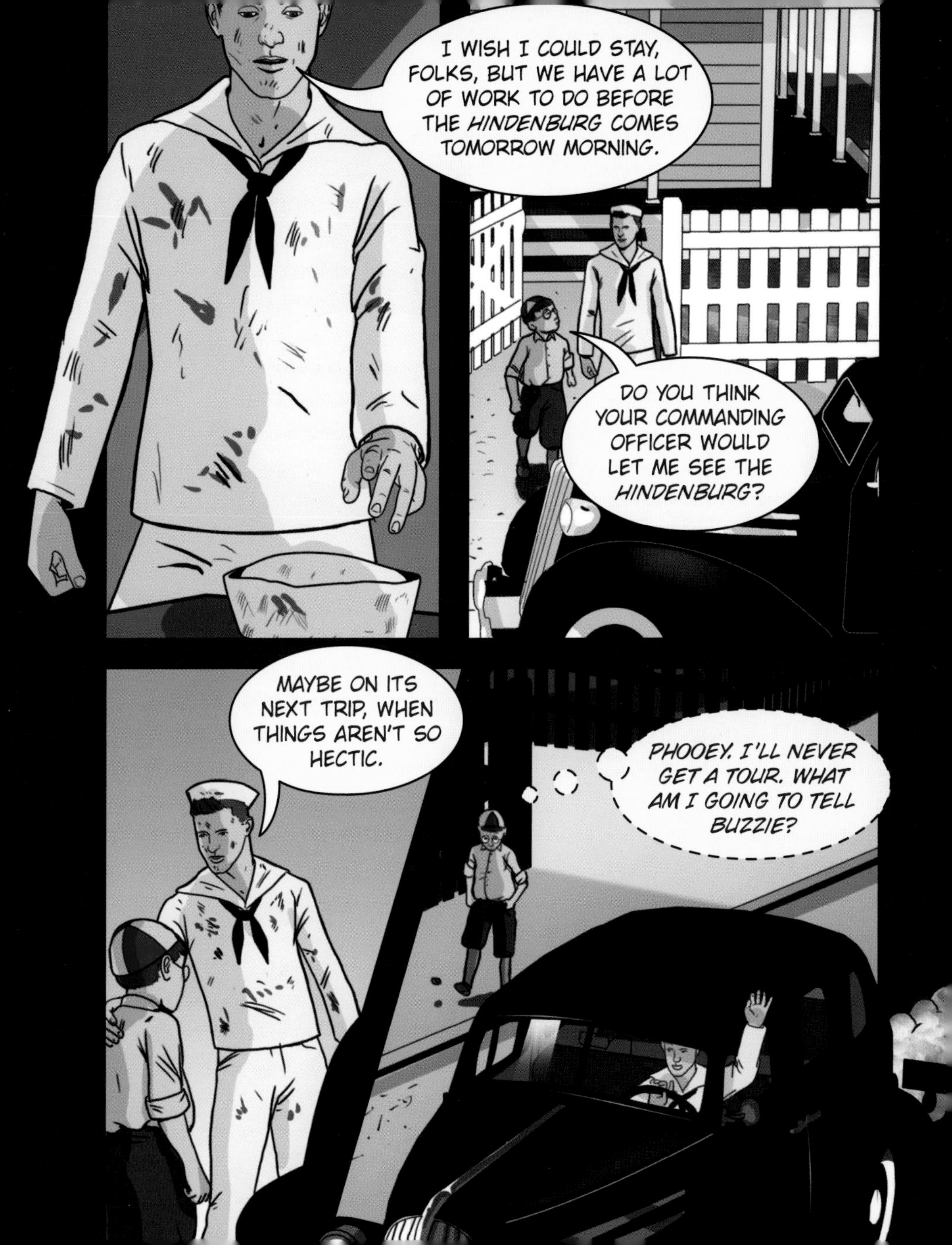
I WISH I COULD STAY, FOLKS, BUT WE HAVE A LOT OF WORK TO DO BEFORE THE *HINDENBURG* COMES TOMORROW MORNING.
DO YOU THINK YOUR COMMANDING OFFICER WOULD LET ME SEE THE *HINDENBURG*?
MAYBE ON ITS NEXT TRIP, WHEN THINGS AREN'T SO HECTIC.
PHOOEY. I'LL NEVER GET A TOUR. WHAT AM I GOING TO TELL BUZZIE?

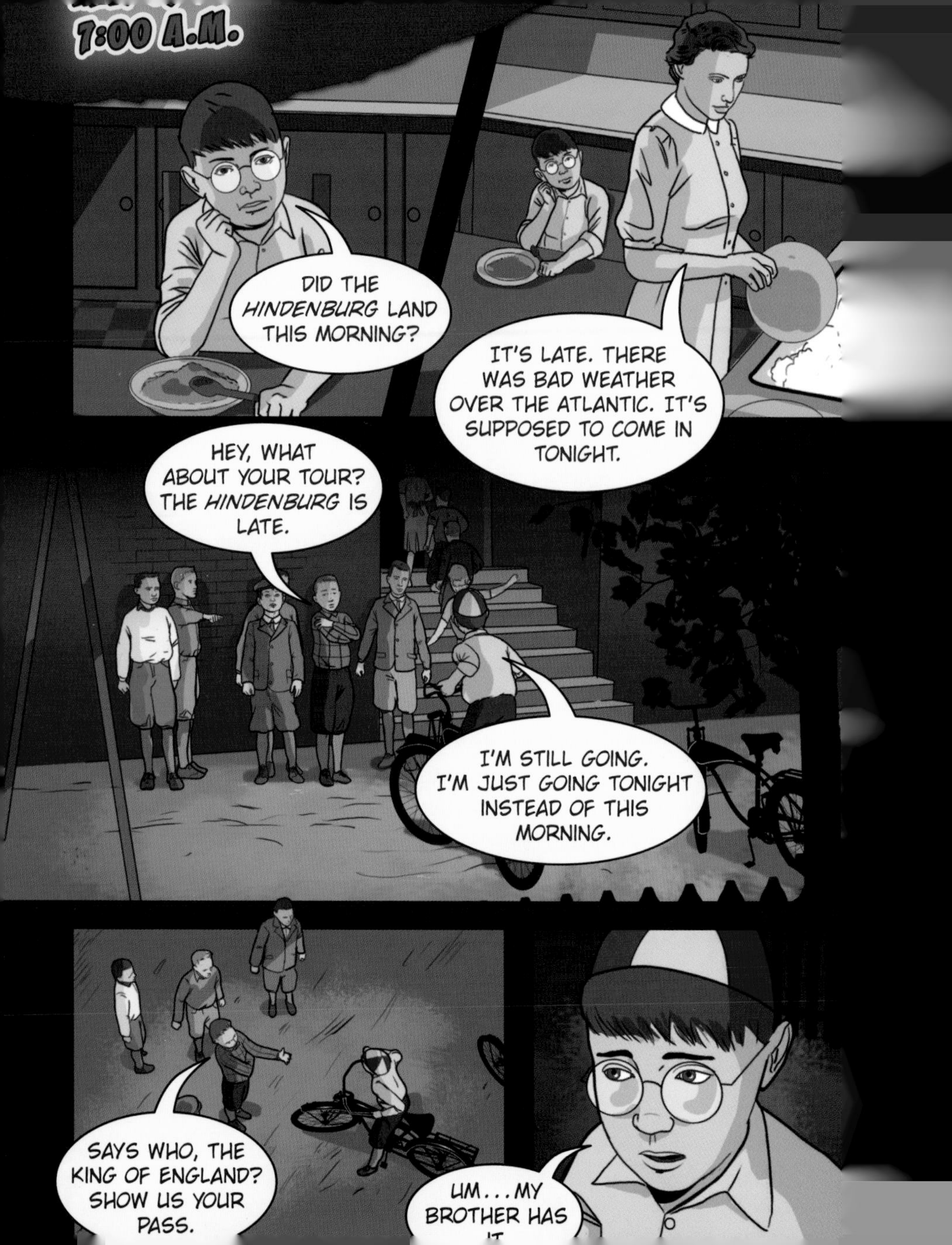
7:00 A.M.
DID THE *HINDENBURG* LAND THIS MORNING?
IT'S LATE. THERE WAS BAD WEATHER OVER THE ATLANTIC. IT'S SUPPOSED TO COME IN TONIGHT.
HEY, WHAT ABOUT YOUR TOUR? THE *HINDENBURG* IS LATE.
I'M STILL GOING. I'M JUST GOING TONIGHT INSTEAD OF THIS MORNING.
SAYS WHO, THE KING OF ENGLAND? SHOW US YOUR PASS.
UM...MY BROTHER HAS

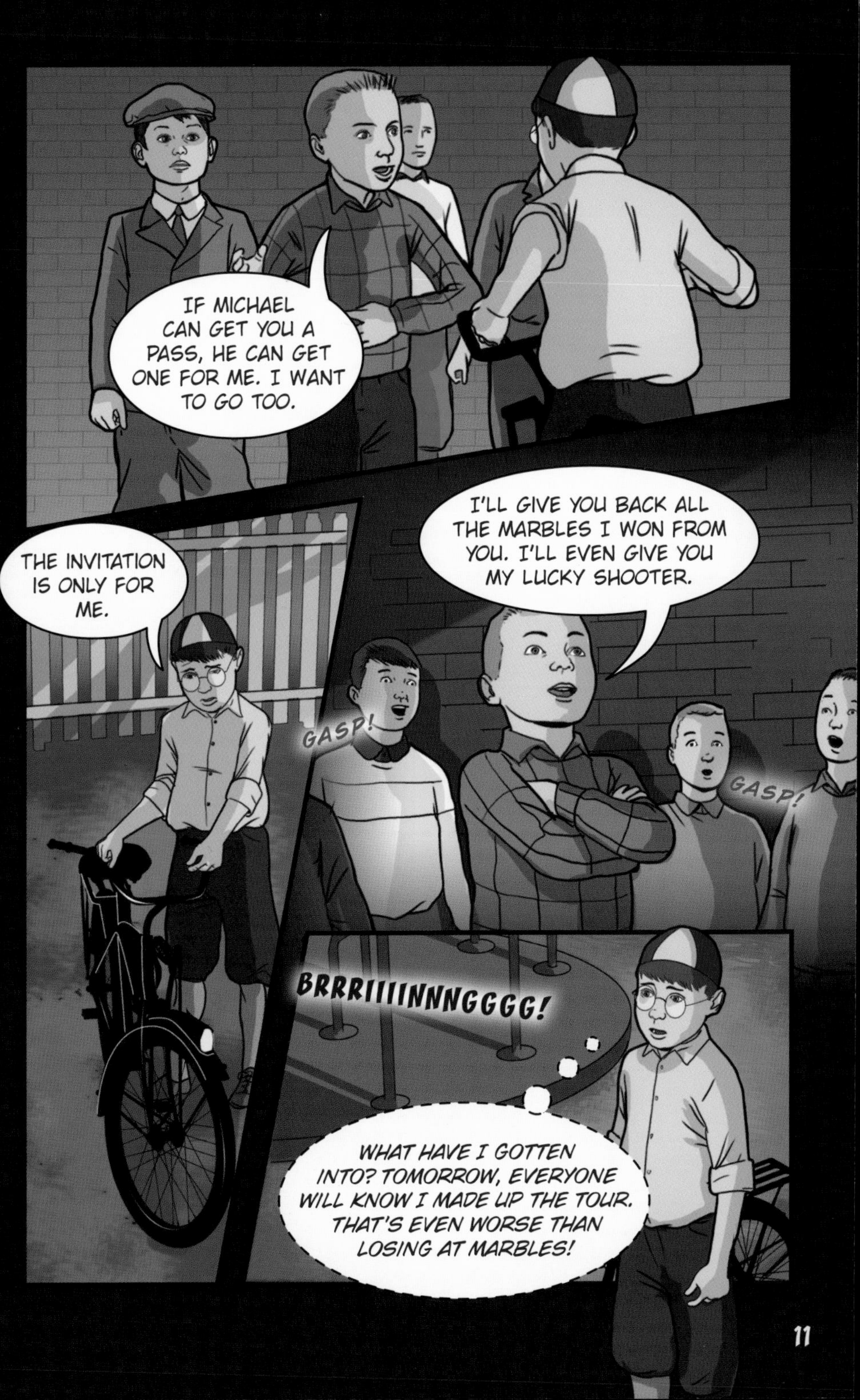
IF MICHAEL CAN GET YOU A PASS, HE CAN GET ONE FOR ME. I WANT TO GO TOO.
THE INVITATION IS ONLY FOR ME.
I'LL GIVE YOU BACK ALL THE MARBLES I WON FROM YOU. I'LL EVEN GIVE YOU MY LUCKY SHOOTER.
GASP!
GASP!
BRRRIIIINNNGGGG!
WHAT HAVE I GOTTEN INTO? TOMORROW, EVERYONE WILL KNOW I MADE UP THE TOUR. THAT'S EVEN WORSE THAN LOSING AT MARBLES!

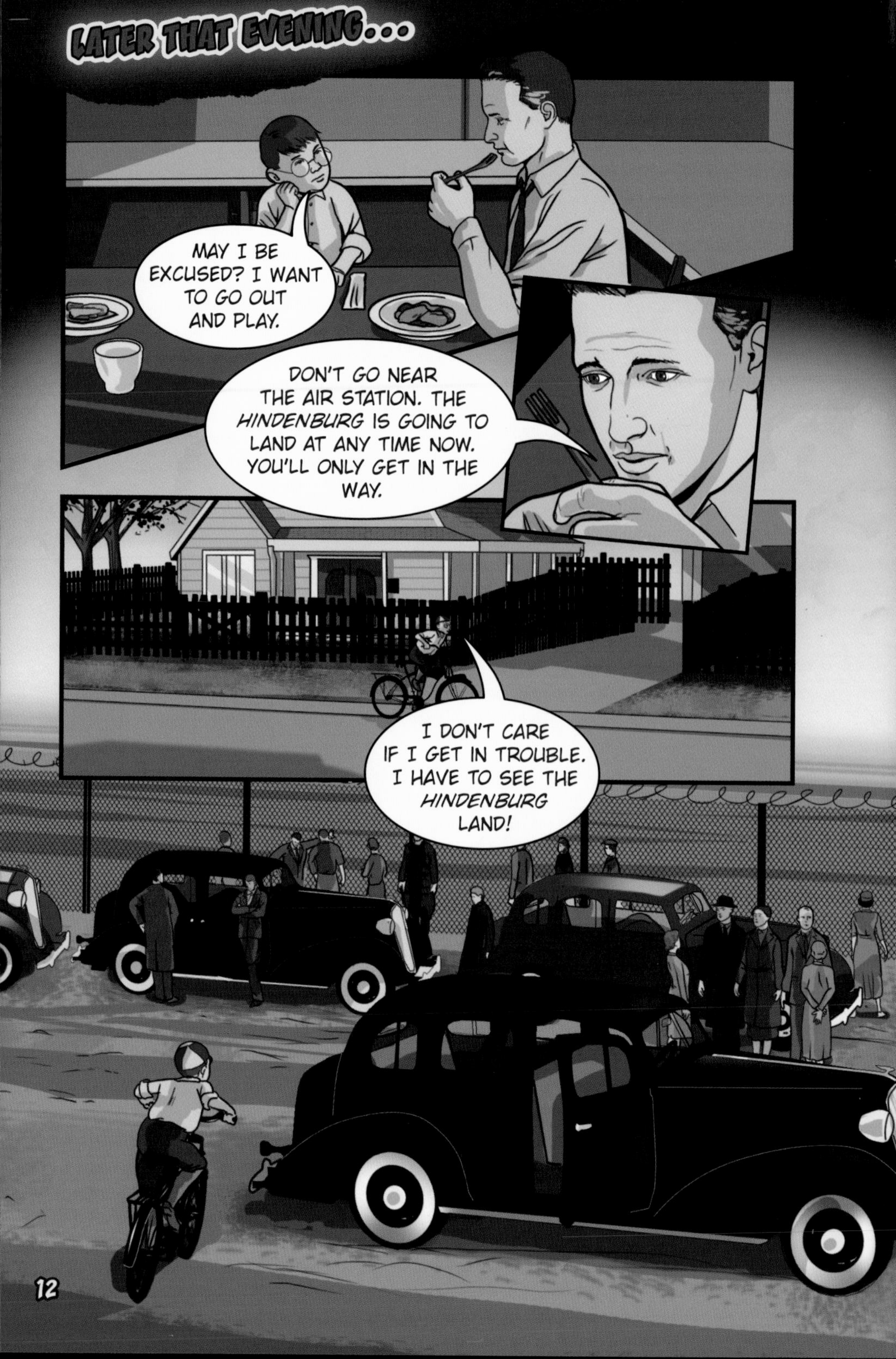
LATER THAT EVENING...
MAY I BE EXCUSED? I WANT TO GO OUT AND PLAY.
DON'T GO NEAR THE AIR STATION. THE *HINDENBURG* IS GOING TO LAND AT ANY TIME NOW. YOU'LL ONLY GET IN THE WAY.
I DON'T CARE IF I GET IN TROUBLE. I HAVE TO SEE THE *HINDENBURG* LAND!

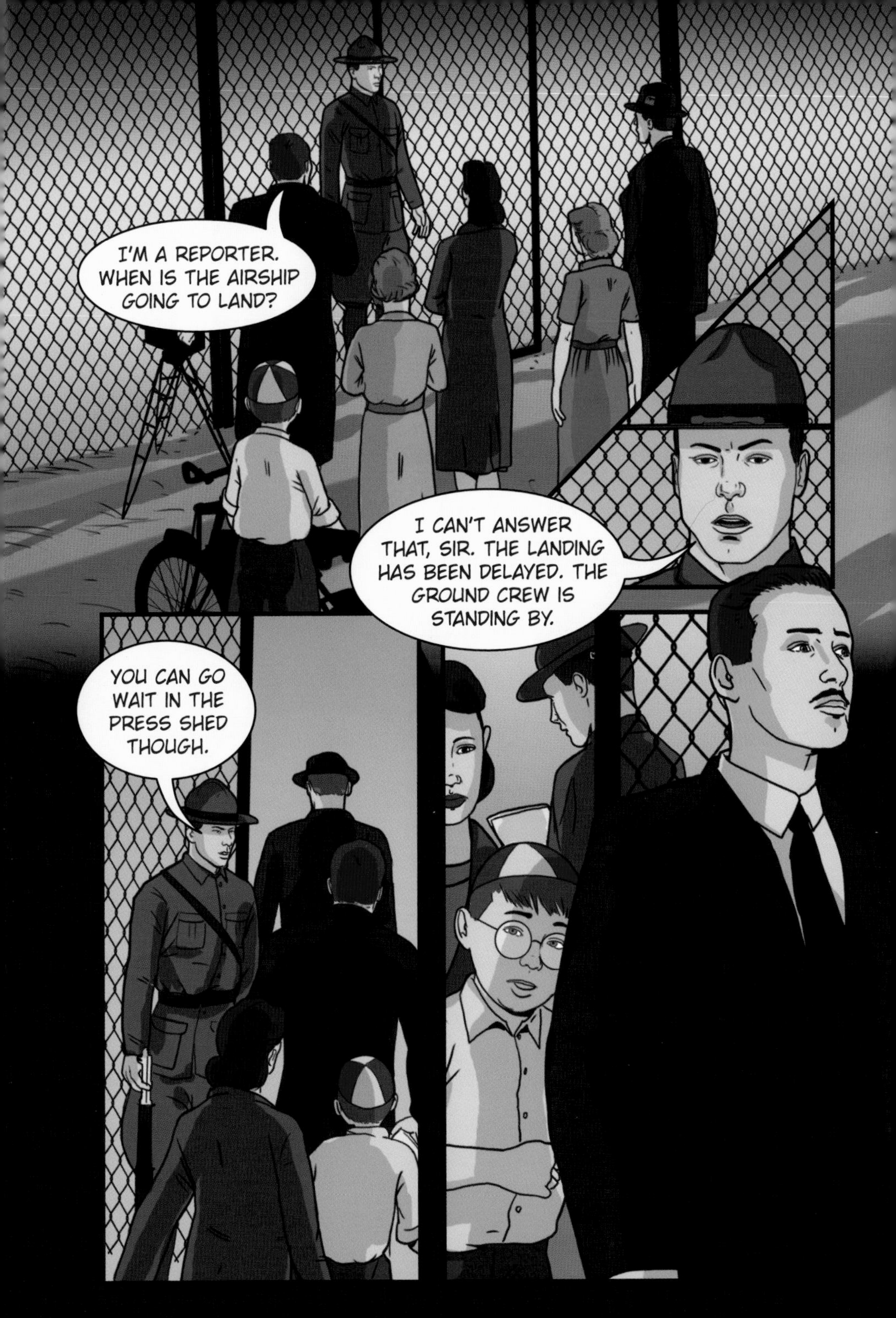
I'M A REPORTER. WHEN IS THE AIRSHIP GOING TO LAND?
I CAN'T ANSWER THAT, SIR. THE LANDING HAS BEEN DELAYED. THE GROUND CREW IS STANDING BY.
YOU CAN GO WAIT IN THE PRESS SHED THOUGH.

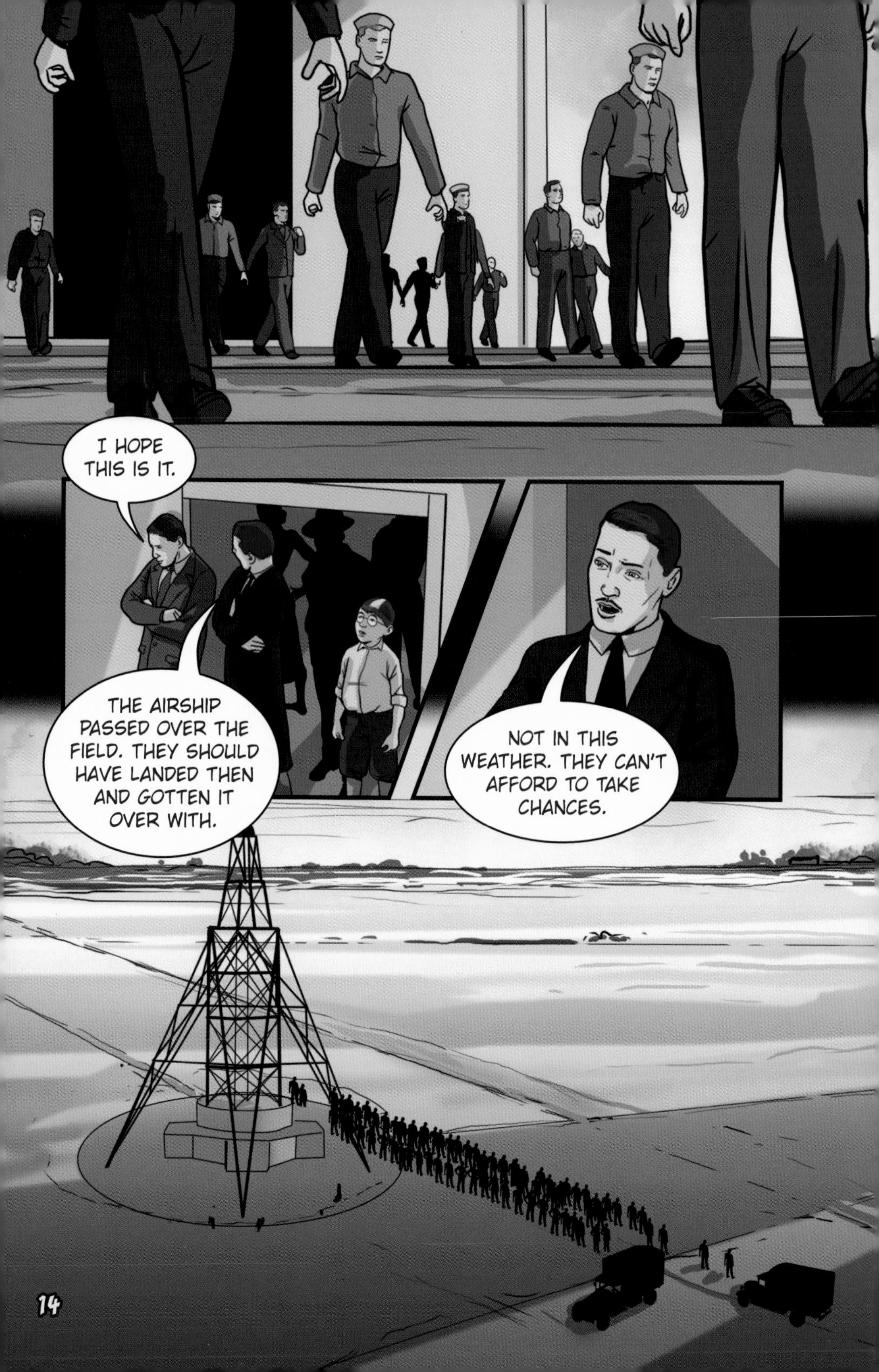
I HOPE THIS IS IT.
THE AIRSHIP PASSED OVER THE FIELD. THEY SHOULD HAVE LANDED THEN AND GOTTEN IT OVER WITH.
NOT IN THIS WEATHER. THEY CAN'T AFFORD TO TAKE CHANCES.

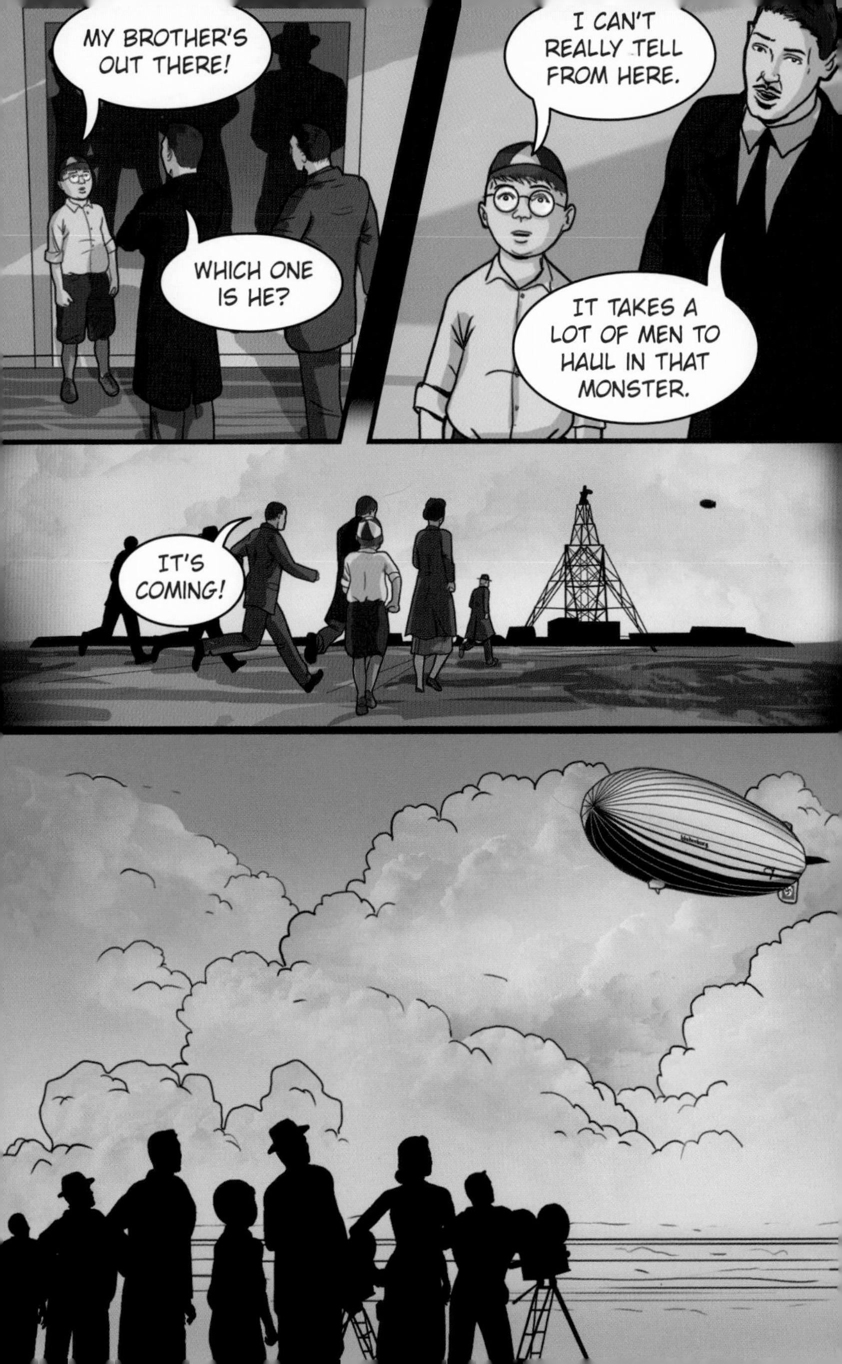
MY BROTHER'S OUT THERE!
WHICH ONE IS HE?
I CAN'T REALLY TELL FROM HERE.
IT TAKES A LOT OF MEN TO HAUL IN THAT MONSTER.
IT'S COMING!

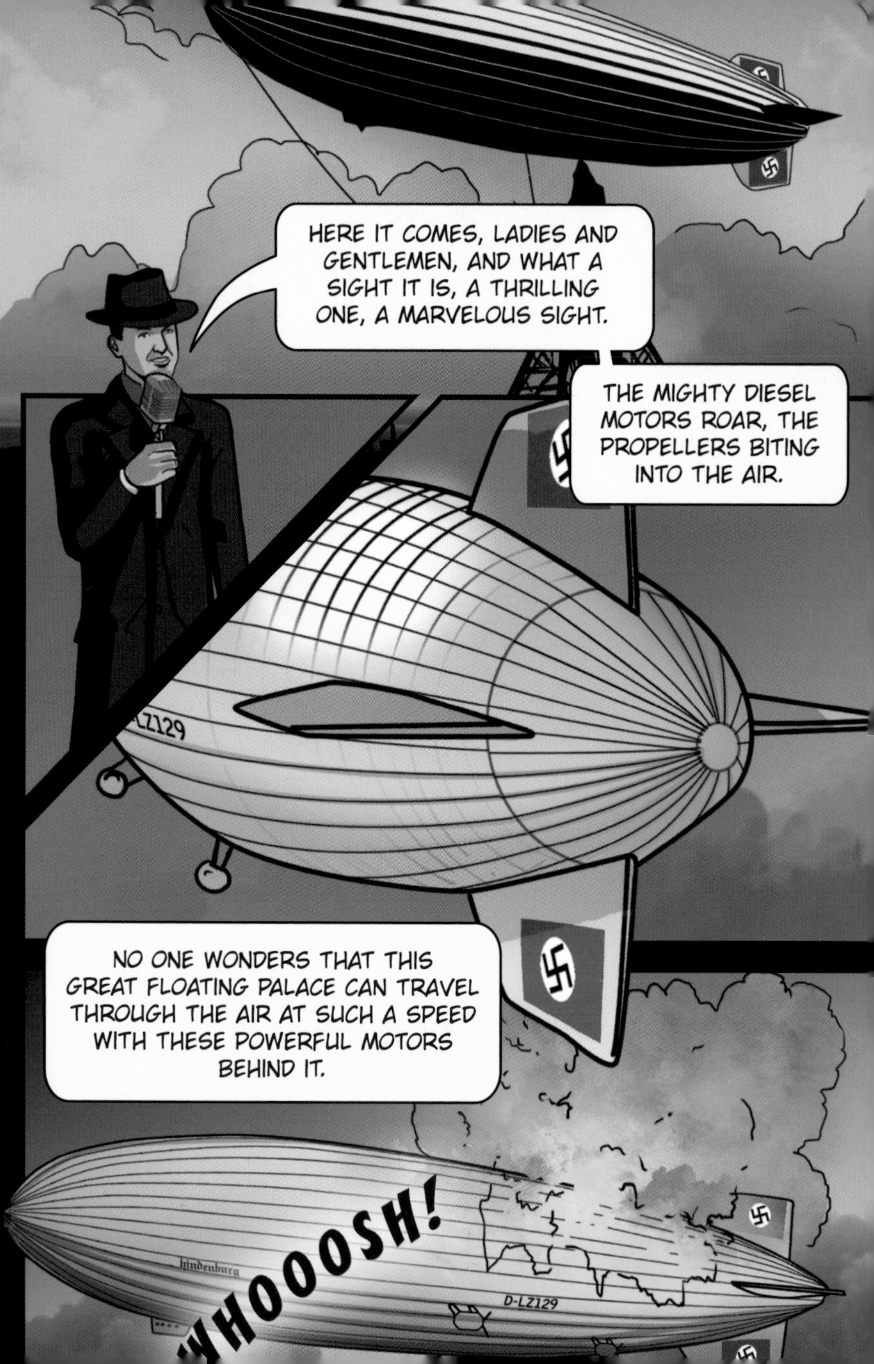
HERE IT COMES, LADIES AND GENTLEMEN, AND WHAT A SIGHT IT IS, A THRILLING ONE, A MARVELOUS SIGHT.
THE MIGHTY DIESEL MOTORS ROAR, THE PROPELLERS BITING INTO THE AIR.
LZ129
NO ONE WONDERS THAT THIS GREAT FLOATING PALACE CAN TRAVEL THROUGH THE AIR AT SUCH A SPEED WITH THESE POWERFUL MOTORS BEHIND IT.
Hindenburg
D-LZ129
WHOOOSH!

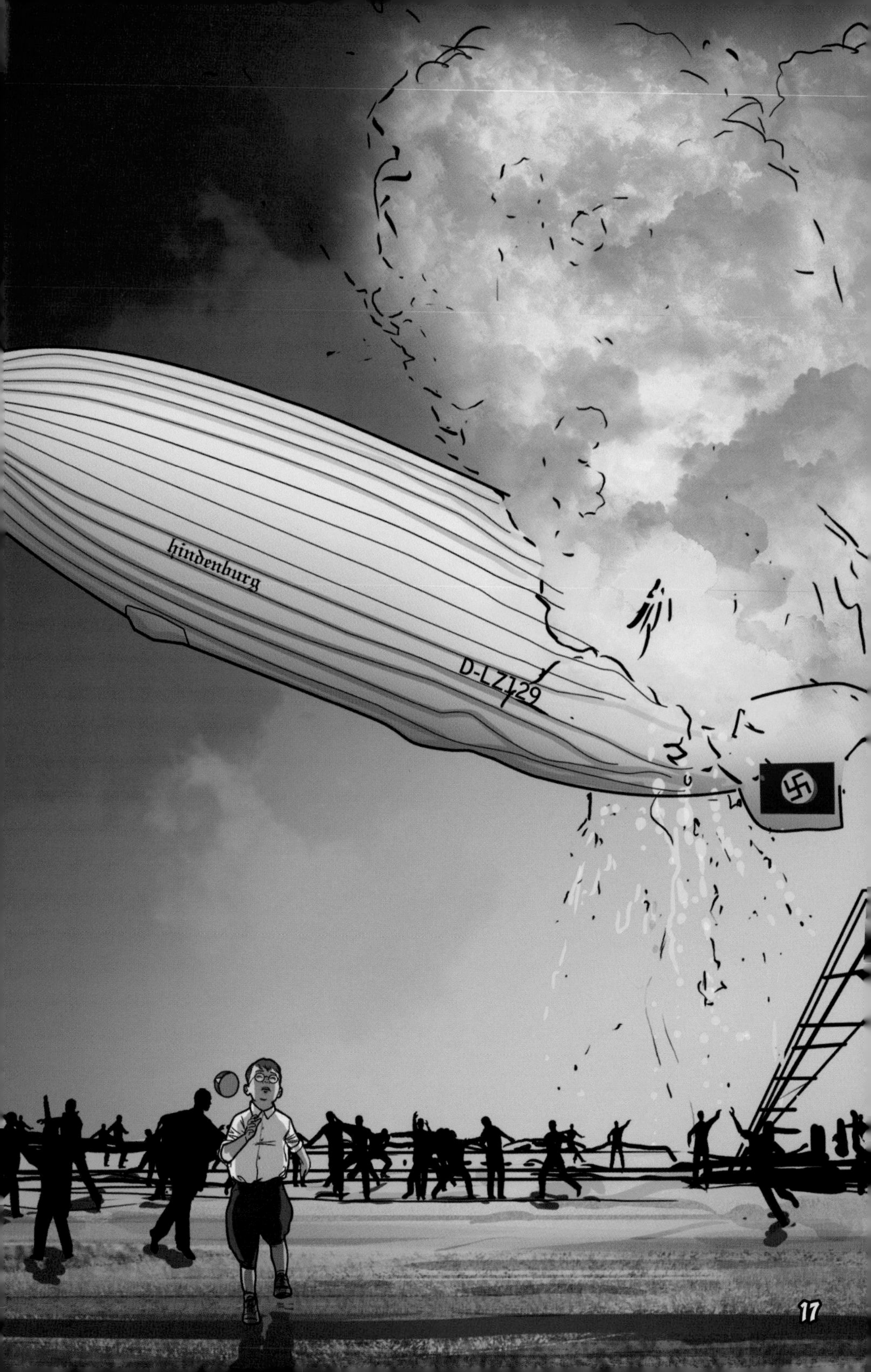
Hindenburg
D-LZ129

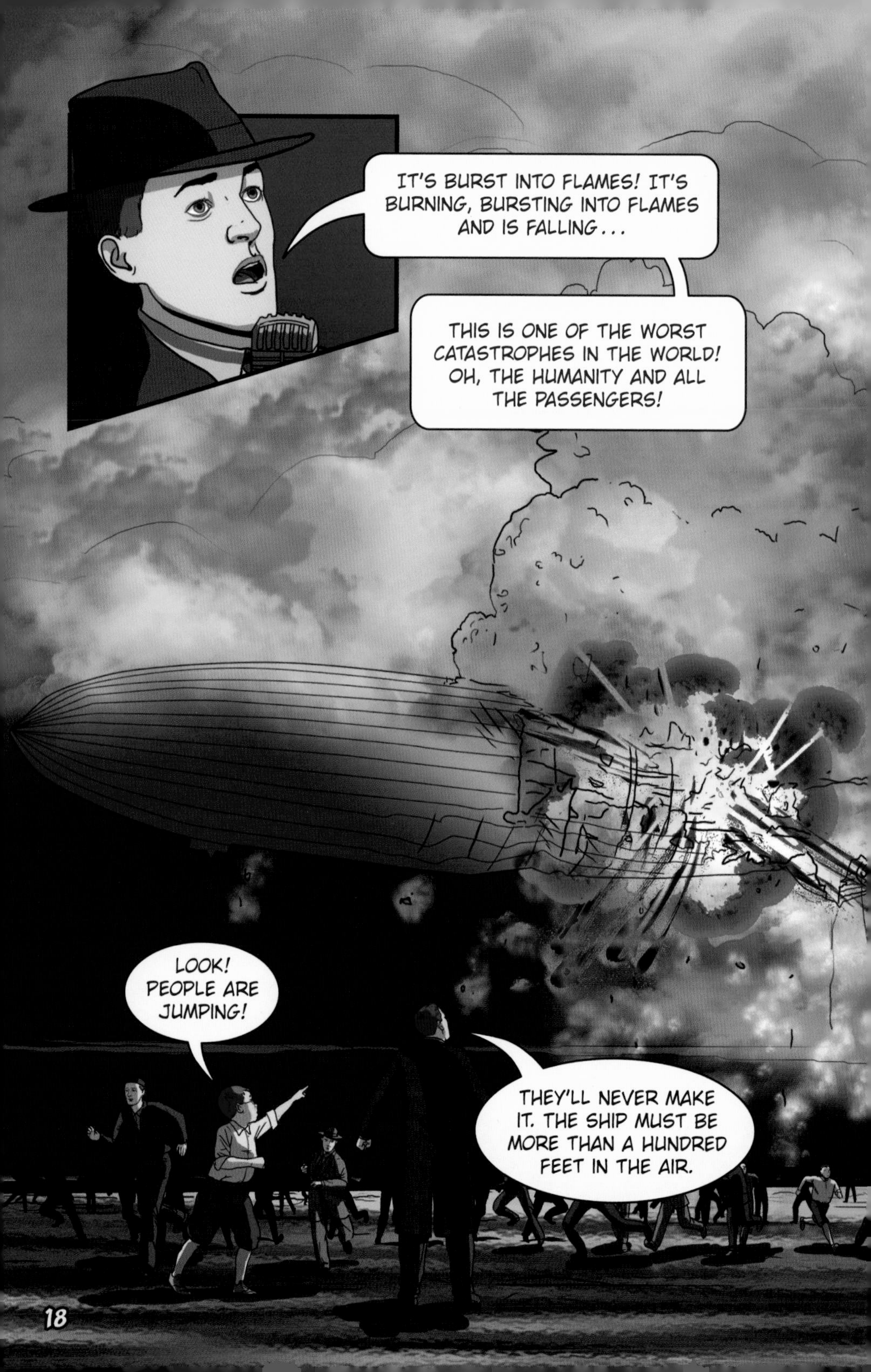
IT'S BURST INTO FLAMES! IT'S BURNING, BURSTING INTO FLAMES AND IS FALLING . . .
THIS IS ONE OF THE WORST CATASTROPHES IN THE WORLD! OH, THE HUMANITY AND ALL THE PASSENGERS!
LOOK! PEOPLE ARE JUMPING!
THEY'LL NEVER MAKE IT. THE SHIP MUST BE MORE THAN A HUNDRED FEET IN THE AIR.

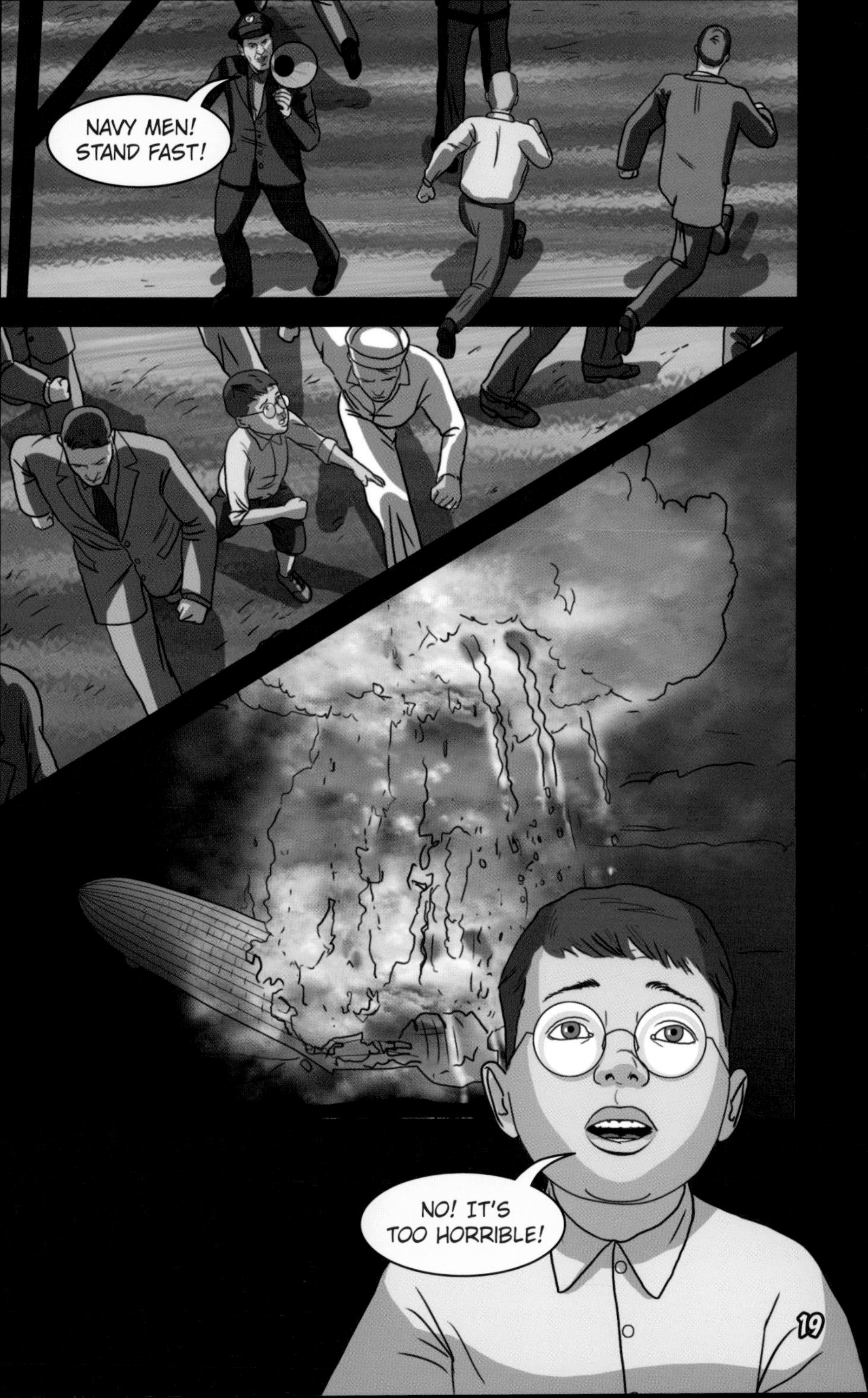
NAVY MEN! STAND FAST!
NO! IT'S TOO HORRIBLE!

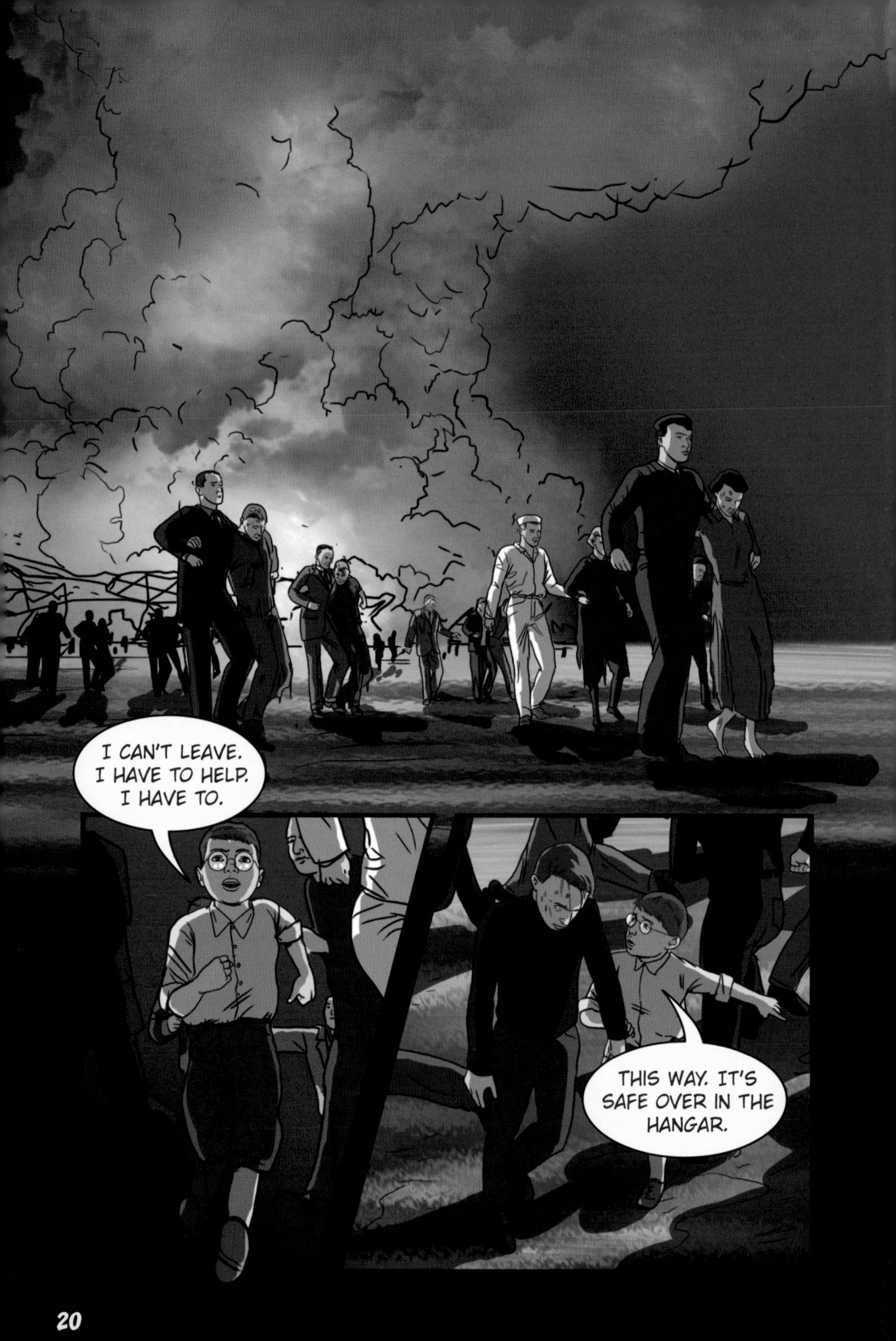
I CAN'T LEAVE. I HAVE TO HELP. I HAVE TO.
THIS WAY. IT'S SAFE OVER IN THE HANGAR.

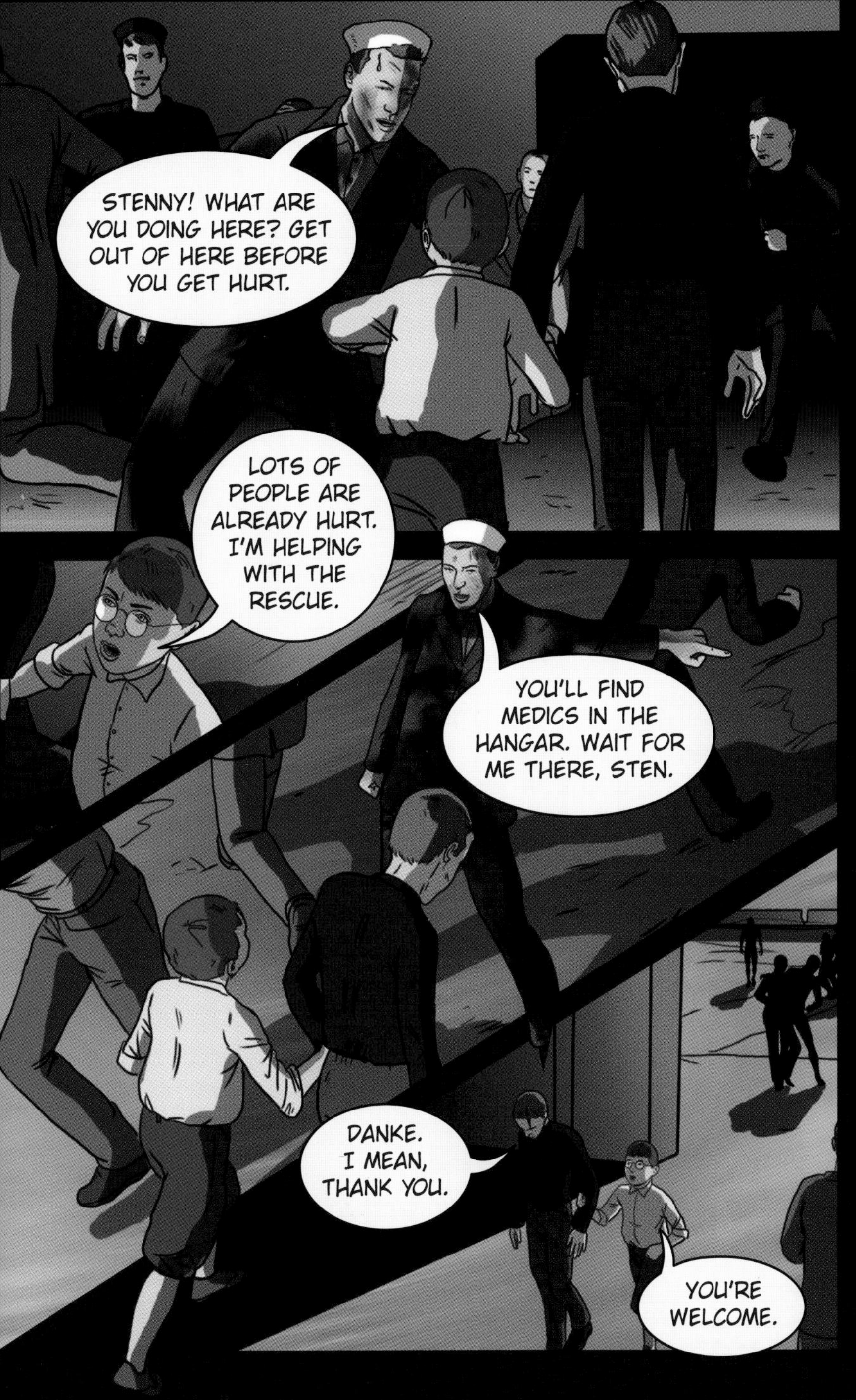
STENNY! WHAT ARE YOU DOING HERE? GET OUT OF HERE BEFORE YOU GET HURT.
LOTS OF PEOPLE ARE ALREADY HURT. I'M HELPING WITH THE RESCUE.
YOU'LL FIND MEDICS IN THE HANGAR. WAIT FOR ME THERE, STEN.
DANKE. I MEAN, THANK YOU.
YOU'RE WELCOME.

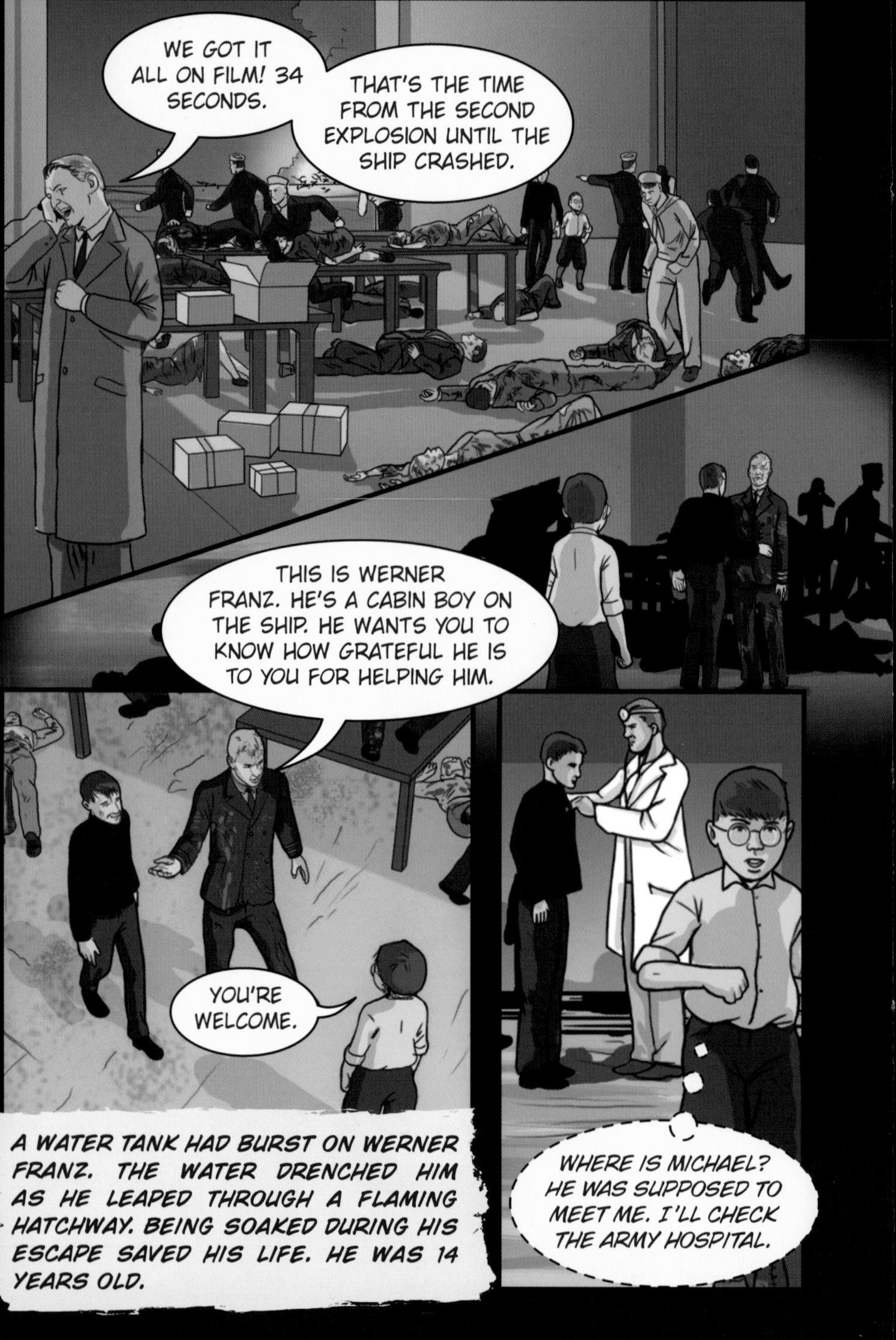
WE GOT IT ALL ON FILM! 34 SECONDS.
THAT'S THE TIME FROM THE SECOND EXPLOSION UNTIL THE SHIP CRASHED.
THIS IS WERNER FRANZ. HE'S A CABIN BOY ON THE SHIP. HE WANTS YOU TO KNOW HOW GRATEFUL HE IS TO YOU FOR HELPING HIM.
YOU'RE WELCOME.
A WATER TANK HAD BURST ON WERNER FRANZ. THE WATER DRENCHED HIM AS HE LEAPED THROUGH A FLAMING HATCHWAY. BEING SOAKED DURING HIS ESCAPE SAVED HIS LIFE. HE WAS 14 YEARS OLD.
WHERE IS MICHAEL? HE WAS SUPPOSED TO MEET ME. I'LL CHECK THE ARMY HOSPITAL.

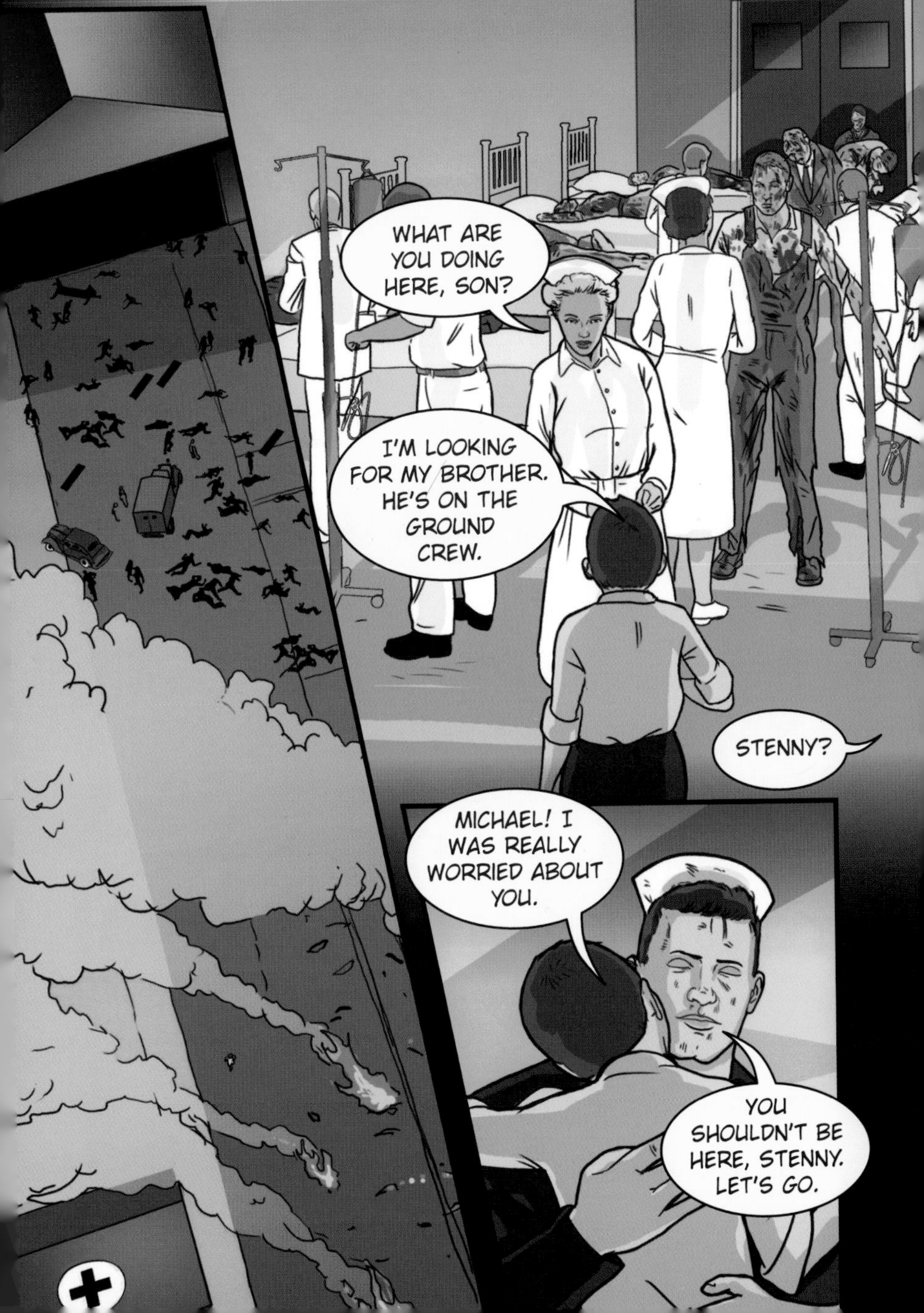
WHAT ARE YOU DOING HERE, SON?
I'M LOOKING FOR MY BROTHER. HE'S ON THE GROUND CREW.
STENNY?
MICHAEL! I WAS REALLY WORRIED ABOUT YOU.
YOU SHOULDN'T BE HERE, STENNY. LET'S GO.

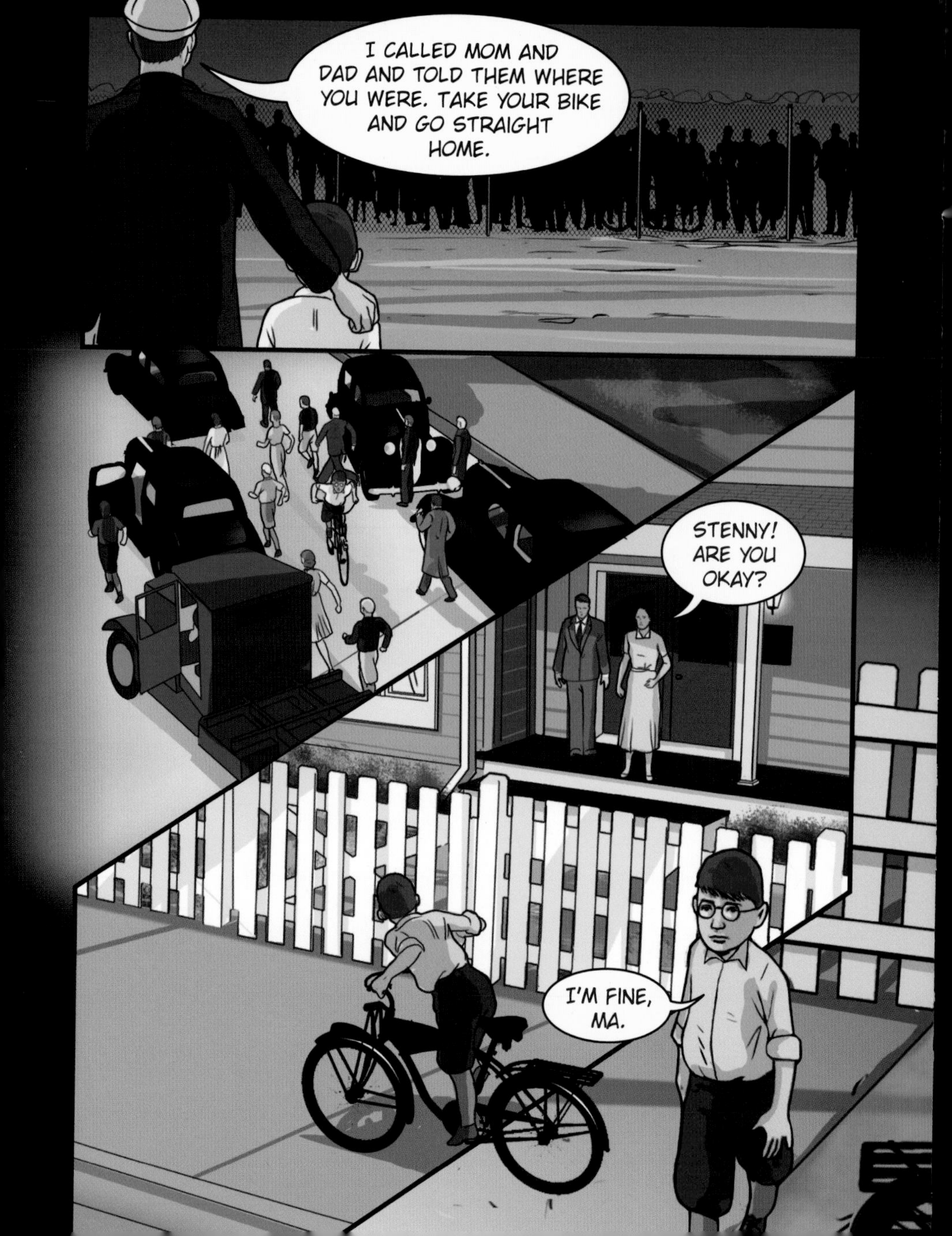
I CALLED MOM AND DAD AND TOLD THEM WHERE YOU WERE. TAKE YOUR BIKE AND GO STRAIGHT HOME.
STENNY! ARE YOU OKAY?
I'M FINE, MA.

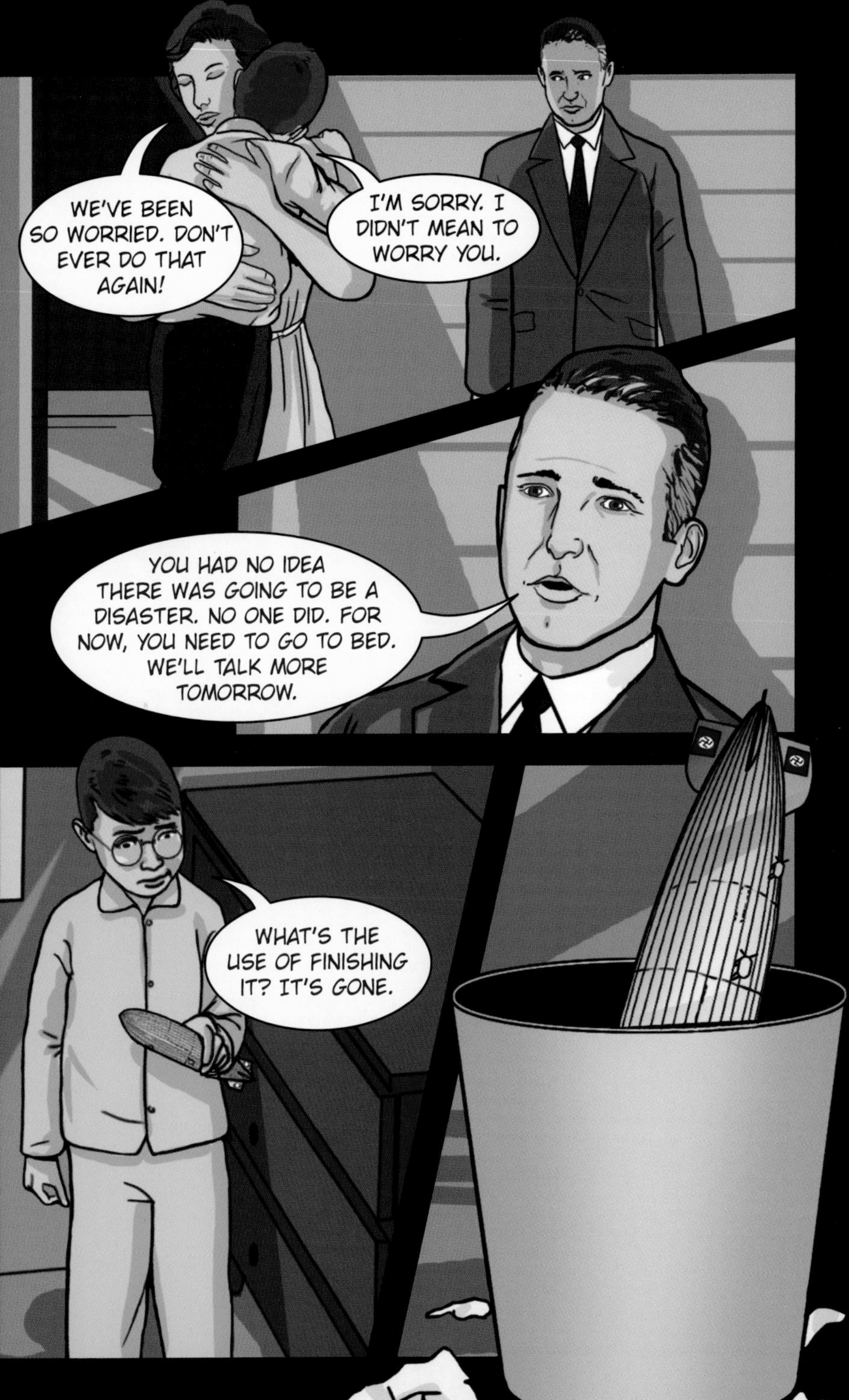

WE'VE BEEN SO WORRIED. DON'T EVER DO THAT AGAIN!
I'M SORRY. I DIDN'T MEAN TO WORRY YOU.
YOU HAD NO IDEA THERE WAS GOING TO BE A DISASTER. NO ONE DID. FOR NOW, YOU NEED TO GO TO BED. WE'LL TALK MORE TOMORROW.
WHAT'S THE USE OF FINISHING IT? IT'S GONE.

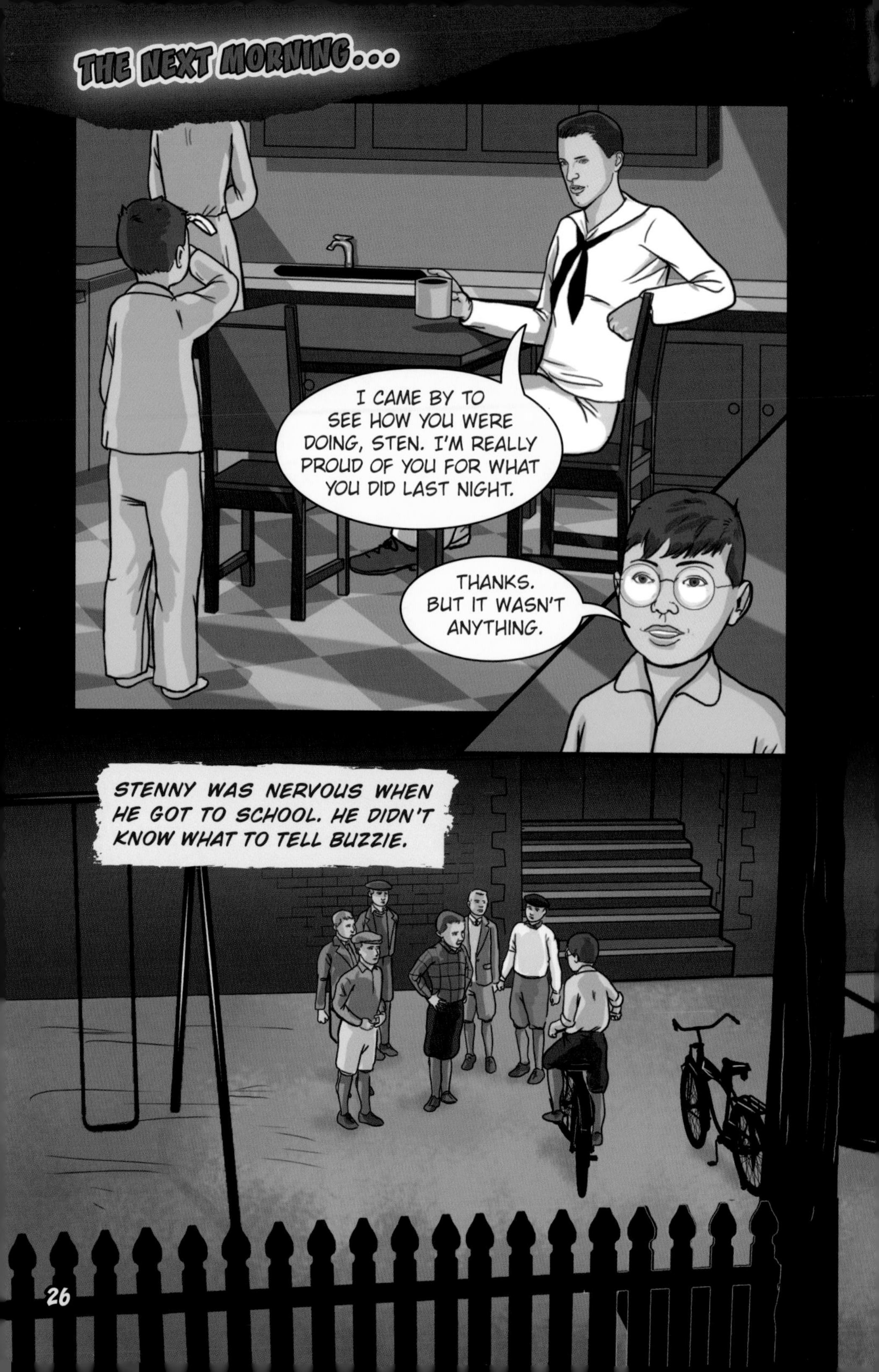
THE NEXT MORNING...
I CAME BY TO SEE HOW YOU WERE DOING, STEN. I'M REALLY PROUD OF YOU FOR WHAT YOU DID LAST NIGHT.
THANKS. BUT IT WASN'T ANYTHING.
STENNY WAS NERVOUS WHEN HE GOT TO SCHOOL. HE DIDN'T KNOW WHAT TO TELL BUZZIE.

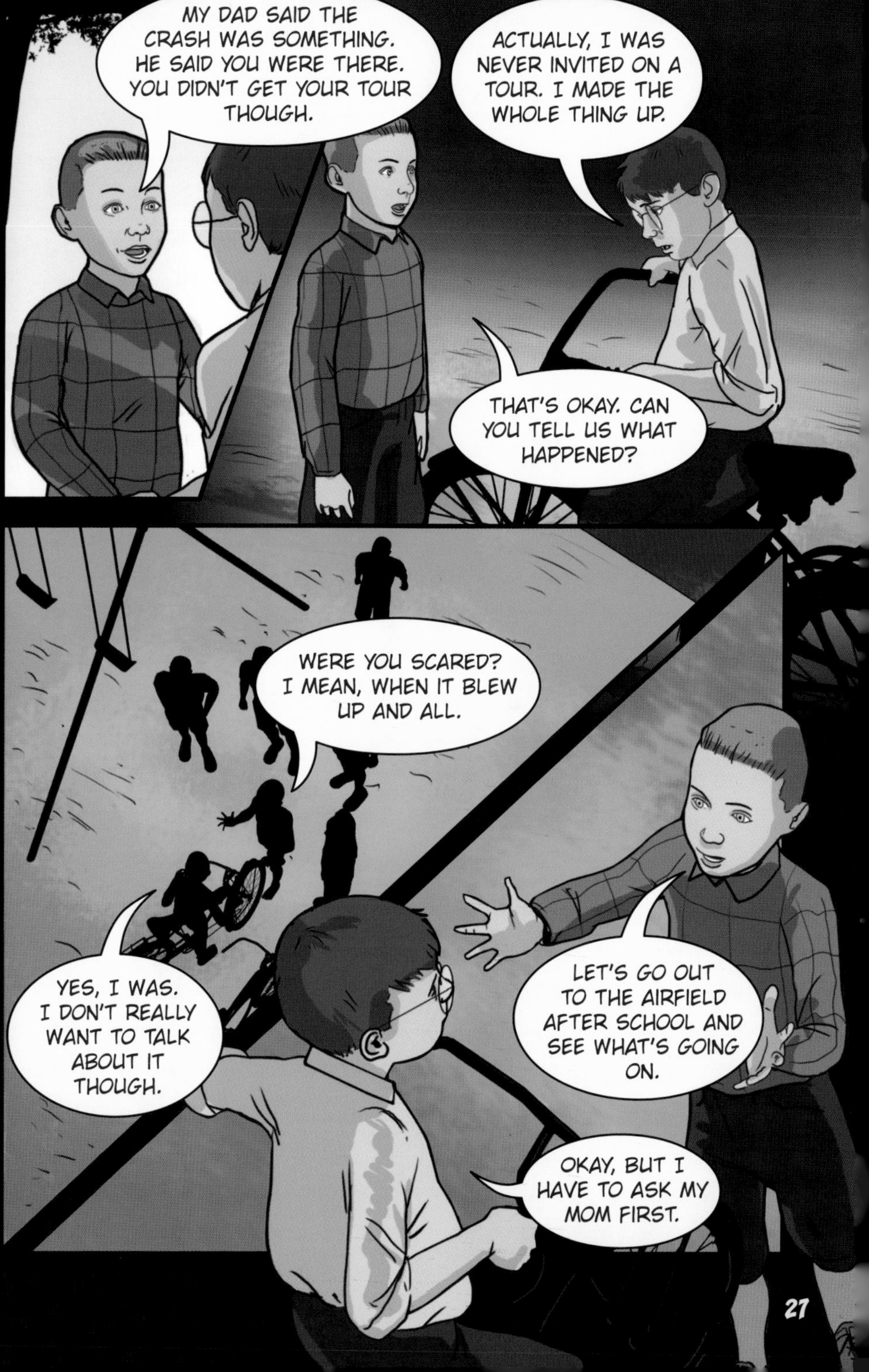

MY DAD SAID THE CRASH WAS SOMETHING. HE SAID YOU WERE THERE. YOU DIDN'T GET YOUR TOUR THOUGH.
ACTUALLY, I WAS NEVER INVITED ON A TOUR. I MADE THE WHOLE THING UP.
THAT'S OKAY. CAN YOU TELL US WHAT HAPPENED?
WERE YOU SCARED? I MEAN, WHEN IT BLEW UP AND ALL.
YES, I WAS. I DON'T REALLY WANT TO TALK ABOUT IT THOUGH.
LET'S GO OUT TO THE AIRFIELD AFTER SCHOOL AND SEE WHAT'S GOING ON.
OKAY, BUT I HAVE TO ASK MY MOM FIRST.

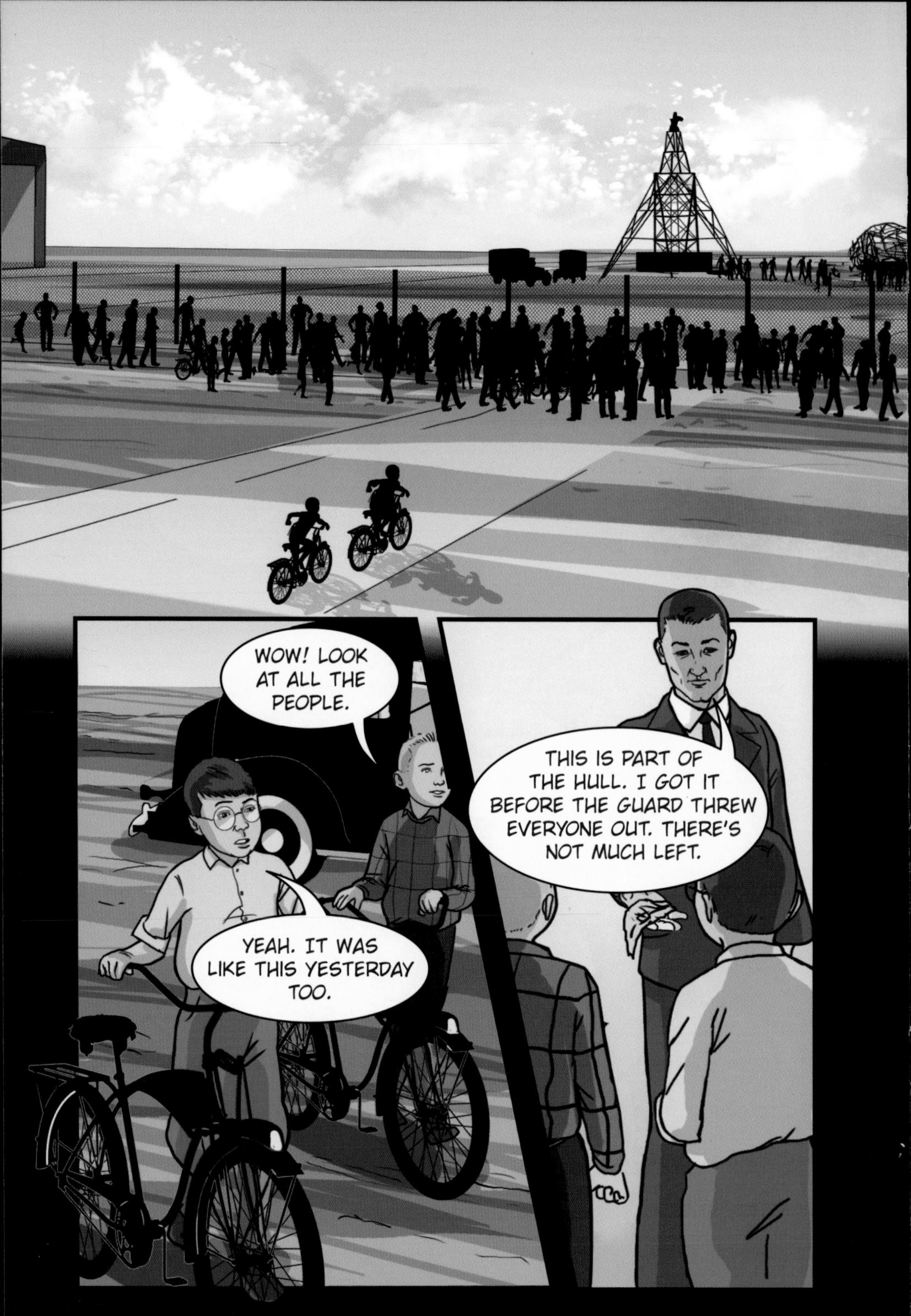
WOW! LOOK AT ALL THE PEOPLE.
YEAH. IT WAS LIKE THIS YESTERDAY TOO.
THIS IS PART OF THE HULL. I GOT IT BEFORE THE GUARD THREW EVERYONE OUT. THERE'S NOT MUCH LEFT.

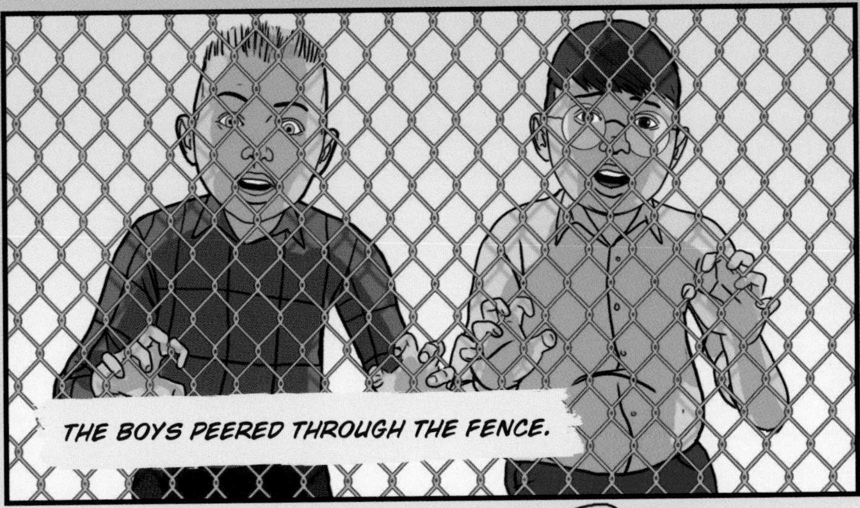
THE BOYS PEERED THROUGH THE FENCE.

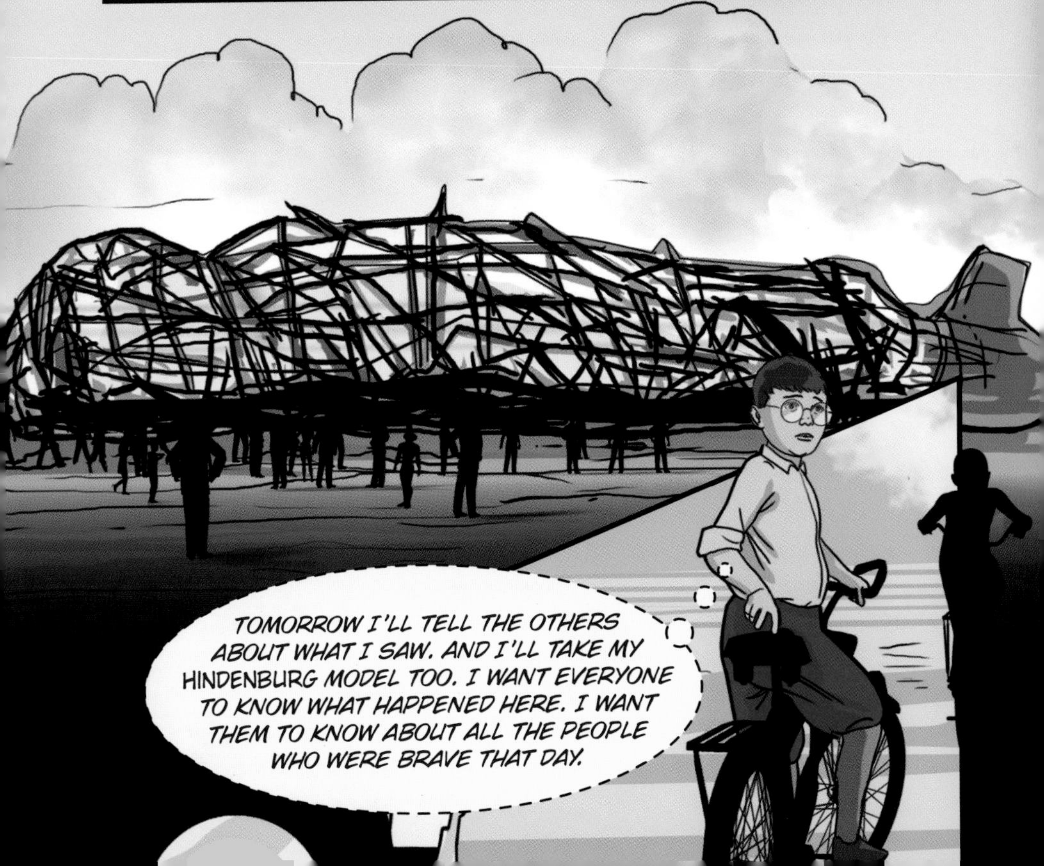
TOMORROW I'LL TELL THE OTHERS ABOUT WHAT I SAW. AND I'LL TAKE MY HINDENBURG MODEL TOO. I WANT EVERYONE TO KNOW WHAT HAPPENED HERE. I WANT THEM TO KNOW ABOUT ALL THE PEOPLE WHO WERE BRAVE THAT DAY.

AFTERWORD

ON ITS FINAL FLIGHT, THE *HINDENBURG* CARRIED 97 PEOPLE, SACKS OF MAIL, AIRPLANE PARTS, A LADY'S DRESS, TWO DOGS, AND THREE PARTRIDGE EGGS.

IN TOTAL, 36 PEOPLE DIED IN THE CRASH: 13 PASSENGERS, 22 AIRSHIP CREWMEN, AND ONE CREWMAN WHO WAS ON THE GROUND. THE OFFICER WHO PILOTED THE AIRSHIP, CAPTAIN PRUSS, SURVIVED. THERE WERE 62 SURVIVORS.

THE CAUSE OF THE CRASH REMAINS A MYSTERY. BEFORE THE VOYAGE, THERE WERE THREATS THAT THE *HINDENBURG* WOULD BE DESTROYED ON U.S. SOIL. BUT NO BOMB FRAGMENTS WERE FOUND IN THE WRECKAGE. OTHER THEORIES INCLUDE STATIC ELECTRICITY OR AN ELECTRICAL FAILURE ON BOARD THE SHIP. WHEREVER IT CAME FROM, A SPARK WAS NECESSARY TO IGNITE THE HYDROGEN INSIDE THE HULL.

THE DISASTER ENDED THE AGE OF AIRSHIPS WITH RIGID BODIES. THE U.S. NAVY AIRSHIP OPERATIONS HAD A POOR TRACK RECORD. THE RIGID DIRIGIBLES *AKRON*, *MACON*, AND THE *SHENANDOAH* HAD ALL CRASHED, KILLING MANY PEOPLE. AFTER THE *HINDENBURG* INCIDENT, THE NAVY SWITCHED TO BLIMPS. THESE NONRIGID AIRSHIPS WERE KEPT ALOFT BY HELIUM, A SAFER, NONFLAMMABLE GAS. THEY PLAYED A SMALL ROLE IN WORLD WAR II (1939–1945). THE U.S. NAVY USED THEM TO FIND ENEMY SUBMARINES ALONG BOTH COASTS OF THE UNITED STATES.

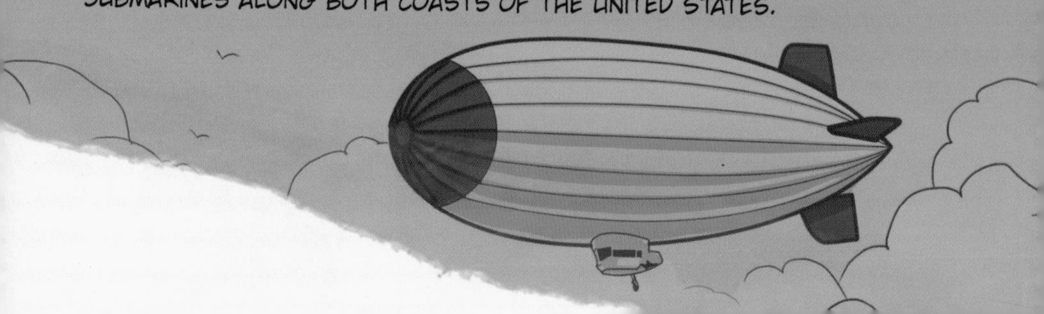

FURTHER READING AND WEBSITES

ADAMS, SIMON. *WORLD WAR II*. NEW YORK: DK PUBLISHING, 2007.

FEIGENBAUM, AARON. *THE* HINDENBURG *DISASTER*. NEW YORK: BEARPORT, 2007.

GRAHAM, IAN. *YOU WOULDN'T WANT TO BE ON THE* HINDENBURG!: *A TRANSATLANTIC TRIP YOU'D RATHER SKIP*. NEW YORK: FRANKLIN WATTS, 2009.

HILL, LEE SULLIVAN. *THE FLYER FLEW!: THE INVENTION OF THE AIRPLANE*. MINNEAPOLIS: MILLBROOK PRESS, 2006.

NASA: HISTORY OF FLIGHT—KID'S PAGE
HTTP://WWW.UEET.NASA.GOV/STUDENTSITE/HISTORYOFFLIGHT.HTML

RICHARDS, JOHN. *AIR AND FLIGHT*. NEW YORK: ALADDIN, 2008.

SCHULZ, WALTER. *JOHNNY MOORE AND THE WRIGHT BROTHERS' FLYING MACHINE*. MINNEAPOLIS: MILLBROOK PRESS, 2011.

TITANIC OF THE SKY: THE *HINDENBURG* DISASTER; VIDEO FOOTAGE AND SLIDESHOW
HTTP://WWW.VIDICOM-TV.COM/TOHIBURG.HTM

ABOUT THE AUTHOR

CANDICE RANSOM HAS WRITTEN MANY AWARD-WINNING FICTION AND NONFICTION BOOKS FOR CHILDREN AND YOUNG ADULTS. SHE HOLDS A MASTER OF FINE ARTS IN WRITING FROM VERMONT COLLEGE. SHE LIVES IN FREDERICKSBURG, VIRGINIA.

ABOUT THE ADAPTER

EMMA CARLSON BERNE HAS WRITTEN AND EDITED MORE THAN TWO DOZEN BOOKS FOR YOUNG PEOPLE, INCLUDING BIOGRAPHIES OF SUCH DIVERSE FIGURES AS CHRISTOPHER COLUMBUS, WILLIAM SHAKESPEARE, THE HILTON SISTERS, AND SNOOP DOGG. SHE HOLDS A MASTER'S DEGREE IN COMPOSITION AND RHETORIC FROM MIAMI UNIVERSITY. BERNE LIVES IN CINCINNATI, OHIO, WITH HER HUSBAND AND SON.

ABOUT THE ILLUSTRATORS

TED HAMMOND IS A CANADIAN ARTIST, LIVING AND WORKING JUST OUTSIDE OF TORONTO. HAMMOND HAS CREATED ARTWORK FOR EVERYTHING FROM FANTASY AND COMIC-BOOK ART TO CHILDREN'S MAGAZINES, POSTERS, AND BOOK ILLUSTRATION.

RICHARD PIMENTEL CARBAJAL HAS A BROAD SPECTRUM OF ILLUSTRATIVE SPECIALTIES. HIS BACKGROUND HAS FOCUSED ON LARGE-SCALE INSTALLATIONS AND SCENERY. CARBAJAL RECENTLY HAS EXPANDED INTO THE BOOK PUBLISHING AND ADVERTISING MARKETS.

Text copyright © 2011 by Candice F. Ransom
Illustrations © 2011 by Lerner Publishing Group, Inc.

Graphic Universe™ is a trademark of Lerner Publishing Group, Inc.

Graphic Universe™
A division of Lerner Publishing Group, Inc.
241 First Avenue North
Minneapolis, MN 55401 U.S.A.

Website address: www.lernerbooks.com

Berne, Emma Carlson.
      The rescue adventure of Stenny Green, Hindenburg crash eyewitness / by Candice Ransom ; adapted by Emma Carlson Berne ; illustrated by Ted Hammond and Richard Pimentel Carbajal.
      p.   cm. — (History's kid heroes)
      Summary: When the huge airship, Hindenburg, catches fire before landing in Lakehurst, New Jersey, in 1937, a nine-year-old eyewitness finds the courage to do what he can to help the victims.
      Includes bibliographical references.
      ISBN: 978–0–7613–6178–7 (lib. bdg. : alk. paper)
      1. Hindenburg (Airship)—Juvenile fiction. 2. Graphic novels. [1. Graphic novels. 2. Hindenburg (Airship)—Fiction. 3. Heroes—Fiction. 4. Ransom, Candice F. 1952- Fire in the sky—Adaptations.] I. Hammond, Ted, ill. II. Carbajal, Richard